GOOD WISH GONE BAD

DON'T MISS THE OTHER STAR DARLINGS BOOKS

Wisher's Guide to Starland

Sage and the Journey to Wishworld
Libby and the Class Election
Leona's Unlucky Mission
Vega and the Fashion Disaster
Scarlet Discovers True Strength
Cassie Comes Through
Piper's Perfect Dream
Astra's Mixed-Up Mission
Tessa's Lost and Found
Adora Finds a Friend
Clover's Parent Fix
Gemma and the Ultimate Standoff

Wish-a-Day Diary

COMING SOON
When We Shine

GOOD WISH GONE BAD

Shana Muldoon Zappa and Ahmet Zappa

with Alexa Young

𝔇𝔦𝔰𝔫𝔢𝔶 PRESS

Los Angeles • New York

Printed in the United States of America
First Hardcover Edition, October 2016
1 3 5 7 9 10 8 6 4 2
FAC-020093-16232
Library of Congress Control Number: 2016936227
ISBN 978-1-4847-5351-4
For more Disney Press fun, visit www.disneybooks.com

SUSTAINABLE Certified Sourcing
FORESTRY
INITIATIVE www.sfiprogram.org
SFI-00993

THIS LABEL APPLIES TO TEXT STOCK

Have you ever wondered what happens when you make a wish?

When you blow out your birthday candles, or toss a coin into a fountain, or pull a wishbone apart, your wish goes out into the universe. But what you probably don't know is that your wish turns into a glowing Wish Orb, invisible to the human eye. This orb travels from Earth on a one-way trip to the brightest star in the sky—Starland.

Starland is inhabited by Starlings, who look a lot like you, except they have a sparkly glow to their skin and hair, and they come in all colors of the rainbow—pink, lavender, you name it! Oh, and one more thing: they have magical powers. Starlings use their magical powers to make good wishes come true, because when good wishes are granted, the result is positive energy—and Starlings need this energy to keep their world running.

There are different types of wishes:

GOOD WISHES: Positive wishes that come from the heart.

Examples: I wish to get an A in math; I wish I could get along with my sister; I wish to be a fashion designer.

Good Wish Orbs are kept in Wish-Houses. Once the time is right for them to be granted, they begin to sparkle. When that happens the orb is presented to the appropriate Starling, who will travel to find the Wisher and help make it come true.

BAD WISHES: Negative wishes meant for selfish, mean-spirited things.

Examples: I wish my friend would fail; I wish I could control people; I wish my enemy would get hurt.

Bad Wish Orbs are transferred to the Negative Energy Facility. They are very dangerous, filled with negative energy, and must not be granted.

IMPOSSIBLE WISHES: These simply can't be granted by Starlings.

Examples: I wish for world peace; I wish all diseases would disappear; I wish my pet hadn't died.

These extra-bright orbs are contained in a special area of the Wish-House, with the hope that one day they might be turned into good wishes that Starlings can help grant.

INSPIRATIONAL WISHES: Wishes for things that haven't been achieved before.

Examples: I wish to be the first female president; I wish to invent a new vaccine; I wish to be the fastest runner in history.

Massive amounts of positive energy are released when these wishes are granted, but even better, they inspire countless other people to wish for things they thought weren't possible. These wishes show us we shouldn't let ourselves be limited by society's expectations!

PRESENT-DAY
STARLAND

Starling Academy was positively glowing. The buildings, the fountains, the trees, and even the moving side-walks—the Cosmic Transporter—looked more dazzling than they had in recent memory. Off in the distance, the Crystal Mountains also appeared to stand a bit taller, prouder, and brighter as the reflection of their multicol-ored peaks bounced off the shimmering azure surface of Luminous Lake below. All signs of the negative wish energy that had been plaguing everything from the fruit orchards to the Starling Academy students themselves had faded away, almost as if the whole crisis had been nothing more than a bad dream—and it was entirely thanks to the Star Darlings!

"Have you ever seen the campus look more beau-tiful?" marveled Sage. Her long lavender braids were also shinier than they had been in quite some time, and they bounced behind her as she and the other Star Darlings hurried past classmates who were heading to the Celestial Café for dinner.

Instead of going to their own evening meal, however, the girls were on their way to Lady Stella's office. The headmistress had summoned them on their Star-Zaps, instructing them to join her right away for an important meeting. In spite of the urgent tone of the holo-text, Sage felt certain that Lady Stella simply wanted to congratulate the Star Darlings again on the successful completion of their top secret Wish Missions. Together, they had collected enough positive wish energy to help ensure that everything on Starland would be powered for countless staryears to come.

"I've never seen the world look more beautiful," said Sage's roommate, Cassie, her eyes widening with delight behind her star-shaped glasses as the girls continued along the Cosmic Transporter.

"It *is* super celestial—but how long do you think this meeting is going to last?" Tessa wondered. "I'm hungry!" Just like her gourmet chef mother, the emerald-haired third-year student was almost always thinking about food.

"Do you think she's got more Wish Missions for us?" asked Libby. It had been a long while since she'd gone on her journey down to Wishworld, and as exciting as it was to know that all twelve Star Darlings had completed their missions, she couldn't wait to go on another one.

"I doubt she'll send us down again so soon," said Scarlet, in her usual surly way, shoving her hands into the front pocket of her sparkling red hoodie and rolling her eyes as the girls made their way into Halo Hall.

A few moments later, they arrived at the door to Lady Stella's office, which was cracked open in anticipation of their visit.

"Girls!" The elegant headmistress stood up from her desk, breathing a sigh of relief as she smoothed down the fabric of her sparkly silver gown. "I thought you'd never get here. Come, let's go down to the Wish Cavern at once."

"I knew it!" Libby tossed her long bubblegum-pink hair proudly and shot a triumphant smile in Scarlet's direction as Lady Stella opened the hidden door in her office wall. Why else would they be going to the Wish Cavern unless she had more missions for them?

The girls followed their headmistress down the secret staircase to the dark caves beneath the school, shivering as they made their way through the chilly air, past the dripping rock formations and toward the door to their own secret Wish-House. It was a special room that had been built exclusively for the Star Darlings and their uniquely powerful Wish Missions.

But unlike the times they'd been in the Wish-House before, this time, at the foot of a large golden waterfall in the gleaming light-soaked room, a round table had been set up with all sorts of treats—including an enormous zoomberry cake and fancy crystal glasses full of sparkling puckerup juice at each place setting. Above the table, a giant holo-banner floated in midair, emblazoned with large, glittery gold letters that spelled out the words CONGRATULATIONS, STAR DARLINGS!

"Well, girls, this is quite a momentous day indeed," Lady Stella began as they all settled into their chairs, which immediately adjusted to their respective heights and weights for optimum comfort. The headmistress raised her tall, delicate glass. "I cannot begin to tell you how pleased I am with what you've each accomplished. Thanks to your hard work and diligence in completing your Wish Missions, there is now more positive wish energy on Starland than ever before!"

The girls all exchanged excited glances, beaming with pride as they, too, raised their glasses and each took a sip. "Star salutations, Lady Stella!" they replied in almost perfect unison.

"And to you," Lady Stella said softly as she cut into the cake, serving each girl a generous slice and encouraging them to eat—which they were more than happy to do. After all, it was highly unusual for young Starlings to be permitted to have dessert before dinner!

As the girls happily chatted, reminiscing about some of the best parts of their missions, Lady Stella glanced around the table at each one of them with a faraway look in her eyes.

"Why aren't you eating?" Tessa asked the headmistress between bites.

Lady Stella pressed her bright red lips together before attempting a smile. But it was no use. She couldn't pretend with them. "Star Darlings . . ." she said, inhaling deeply and closing her eyes for a moment. "We do have much to celebrate—but I suppose I should also tell you that even greater challenges may lie ahead for us all."

The celebratory mood in the air suddenly became thick with nervous energy. What was the headmistress referring to, exactly?

"As you know, everyone at Starling Academy was completely deceived by Lady Cordial, who was our director of admissions. She was someone I trusted and valued as one of my closest confidantes." Lady Stella sighed and shook her head as she stared down at the table. "I genuinely believed that she was our friend—but in fact, she was not Lady Cordial at all. She was Rancora in disguise."

As soon as Lady Stella mentioned that dreaded name, the golden light in the Wish Cavern flickered and dimmed ever so slightly, and the Star Darlings all felt an icy chill run down their spines. They frowned and nodded solemnly. Although they had managed to avoid discussing Lady Cordial for the past week, they of course knew that at some point her name—and the far more terrifying name of Rancora—would come up again. They had simply hoped it wouldn't be quite so soon.

"But she's gone now," Gemma pointed out, her wavy orange ponytail glimmering.

"Well, yes, she has left Starling Academy—that's true," Lady Stella acknowledged. "However, we don't know *where* she's gone or what she might be planning to do next. So although I'm hopeful that she'll keep her distance and stay far, far away from the school grounds, I believe that she may be planning something bigger— something that will place Starland in even greater danger."

"Wh-what could be more dangerous than the negative energy she was releasing?" asked Cassie, who began trembling so much that she had to set down her fork.

"Yeah—and how much more can she really do?" Vega wondered. "You said that there's more positive wish energy on Starland than ever before—plus, we already defeated her when we united our twelve Power Crystals.

Won't that be enough to stop Rancora again, even if she tries to do something else?"

"That is my hope—but I'm still trying to find the missing page that I believe Rancora, or rather Lady Cordial, stole from the oracle," Lady Stella replied, referring to the ancient text that foretold of the twelve girls and the role they would play in saving Starland. "While I spend the next few days continuing my search, I suggest that you all put this out of your minds and get some rest. You've been through so much and will need your energy—not only for your studies, but in the event that I require your assistance again. Of course, that will depend on what I'm able to find out."

While the girls quietly pondered everything Lady Stella had said, she tried to encourage them to continue their celebration, offering them more cake and juice. But Tessa was the only one who still had any sort of an appetite left.

"I'm sorry, girls," Lady Stella said with a frown. "I hadn't intended to bring this up with you today—but it's important for you to be aware of the potential challenges that may lie ahead. Try not to worry too much. I *will* come up with a solution."

"We know you will," said Libby, her bright pink eyes gleaming with positive energy. "And we can help as soon as you need us!"

"Yes!" agreed Clover, lightly tapping the rim of her purple fedora. "We'll do whatever it takes. Right, Star Darlings?"

"Right!" the girls all cheered.

But as they got up from their comfy chairs and shuffled out of the Wish-House, the mood was anything but cheery.

The next morning, every last one of the Star Darlings woke up early. In fact, most of them had hardly slept at all. Vega had been especially restless, plagued by nightmares about Rancora, with her piercing purple eyes and ashen skin and hair, the blazing pink collar of her long, tattered gray gown rising behind her head like the fiery flames of doom. Sitting up in bed, Vega leaned back against her headboard and began to record holo-notes on her Star-Zap about everything she had observed about Lady Cordial. She still couldn't believe that the frumpy-dumpy director of admissions had been the evil Rancora in disguise all that time!

"You couldn't sleep, either?" Piper asked in a soft ethereal voice from her side of the room as she pushed off her cozy aqua comforter and pulled her long seafoam-green hair up into a high ponytail.

"No." Vega rubbed her blue eyes and shook her

head. Her chin-length cobalt bob looked perfect as ever, in spite of the fact that she was still in bed. "I can't stop thinking about Lady Cordial—or, you know, *Rancora*. I should have realized that she might still be plotting something terrible."

"I know." Piper slid on her fluffy slippers, closed her eyes, and took several deep, cleansing breaths. "I've been having visions ever since Lady Stella mentioned her name yesterday."

Vega wrinkled her nose. Sometimes Piper's visions could be kind of out there—but other times they had proven to be right on target. "What kind of visions?"

"Well . . ." Piper took a few more deep breaths. "It's kind of scary."

"Tell me!" Vega demanded.

"All right. I saw Rancora in a big dark cloud—but she kept changing into Lady Cordial and then back into herself again," Piper recounted. "Every time she changed into Rancora, she tried to pull us into the cloud, too, and she kept saying she wanted us to join forces with her."

"Us—who is *us*?" Vega's eyes darkened with worry.

"All twelve of us—the Star Darlings," Piper said.

"Oh, my stars!" Vega jumped out of bed and began pacing around the room. "What if you're right? What if she tries to turn us into her negative energy minions?

Her toxic trainees! We need to figure out exactly what Rancora is planning and find a way to stop her—like, *now.*"

Piper widened her eyes, mystified by Vega's words. "But Lady Stella said she was going to search for the missing page from the oracle and *then* figure out what needs to be done. She told us we needed to wait to hear from her. She said we needed to rest up so we could get our energy back."

"I know," Vega said tersely. "But I don't want to sit around waiting—or resting—when we could be helping. We don't want to be caught off guard, right? The more prepared we are, the better!"

Piper shrugged and sat back in bed while Vega raced around her side of the room, grabbing her toothlight and rushing out to take a sparkle shower. Within minutes, she was back and getting dressed in a shiny blue blazer over a matching tunic, paired with sparkly tights and ankle boots.

"What are you going to do?" Piper asked.

"We need to go to the Illumination Library!" Vega informed her.

"The library? Why?" Piper looked blankly at her roommate.

"So we can try to figure out exactly where Rancora came from," Vega explained. "There's *got* to be a holo-book there that will point us in the right direction! Hurry up and get ready. I'll holo-text everyone to meet us there!"

"Okay," Piper agreed reluctantly.

A few of the Star Darlings were already out in front of the Illumination Library when Vega and Piper showed up, some looking more awake than others.

"What's this all about?" asked Adora, who was flaw-lessly styled, as usual, in shimmering indigo leggings with knee-high boots and a chic fitted dress, her pale blue hair piled high in a fashionably messy updo.

"Yeah, what's happening?" echoed Adora's room-mate, Tessa, stifling a yawn as she popped the last bite of a glorange spice muffin into her mouth.

"I'll tell you when the others get here," Vega replied, tapping her foot as she stared impatiently across the Star Quad. Finally, she could see the rest of the girls moving toward the library on the Cosmic Transporter.

"What's up?" Libby asked when she arrived. "We got here as fast as we could!"

"Piper and I were up all night, thinking about the whole Lady Cordial—*Rancora*—situation," Vega explained as the others all gathered round. "Piper had a vision that Lady Cordial kept turning into Rancora and was trying to pull us into some sort of dark cloud, insist-ing she wanted us to join forces with her or something."

"Seriously?" Scarlet crossed her arms in frustration. "You called us all the way here to tell us *that?*"

"No." Vega glared at Scarlet, whose short fuchsia hair was slightly messy from sleep. "I called you here because obviously there's a lot more to Rancora than any of us realize, and we need to know more about her if we're going to figure out what she might be planning to do to us—or to Starland—next. Lady Stella may be doing her research, but I think we should start doing a bit of our own, too!"

"What kind of research?" asked Libby, always eager to help in any way she could.

"Well, for starters we should see what we can find out about Lady Cordial, since that's who Rancora was in disguise," Vega proposed.

"That's not a bad idea," Sage noted. "There's got to be some information about her in the faculty pages of the school staryearbooks."

"Exactly!" Vega agreed.

"I don't see how that's going to help," Scarlet protested. "What are the staryearbooks going to tell us that we—and especially Lady Stella—don't already know?"

"I say we give it a try," Leona chimed in, giving her shiny golden curls a confident pat. "If we *do* find out something useful, Lady Stella will think we're even bigger stars than we already are."

"I agree," said Sage.

"Me too." Tessa nodded.

"Ugh. Fine." Scarlet rolled her eyes, giving in after all the others had voiced their support as well.

"Excellent," Vega said with a smile, leading the way into the library.

With most of the Starling Academy campus still asleep, it was even quieter inside than usual. The twelve girls made their way through the vast stacks of holo-books and up the winding staircase to the section where the staryearbooks were located. The tomes contained holo-images of every student and faculty member who had ever been at Starling Academy, along with detailed records of everything that had happened during each school staryear since the very first class had enrolled.

"So what are we looking for, exactly?" asked Gemma, accessing the pages of a recent staryearbook as she sat down on a plush orange couch and then beginning to scan through them. "This says Lady Cordial has been at Starling Academy for two years and she's helped to make the school what it is today."

"Ha—only because nothing's been written about *us* yet!" Leona grinned proudly while Vega sat down next to Gemma and tapped on the image of Lady Cordial, eager to see if anything more useful might pop up.

Alas, all she saw was the director of admissions

shuffling from her office to Lady Stella's office, then back to her office, with an occasional moment where she spilled something or tripped. *That* was helping to make the school what it was today?

"There has to be more information about her than this," Vega said with a frown, taking the book from Gemma and scrolling through it some more.

"I'm kind of with Scarlet—even if we found more information about Lady Cordial, what would it really tell us?" asked Adora, sitting down next to Vega. "Isn't *Rancora* the one we need to investigate?"

"Yes, but they're one and the same," Vega pointed out as she continued to scroll through the pages, moving farther and farther back through the book.

"True, but we might find something more informative—something she was hiding—if we go to her office, or maybe even her old residence in StarProf Row," Adora pointed out.

"Adora's probably right," Sage agreed.

"She's *totally* right!" Scarlet said.

"Oh, my stars!" Piper suddenly called out. She had wandered off and found a much older staryearbook, which she was now gazing at in wide-eyed wonder.

"What?" Vega asked, leaping up from the couch and racing over to grab the holo-book from her roommate before returning to the couch with it.

"What is it, Vega?" Sage asked, positioning herself behind Vega so she could get a better view.

"It's . . . it's . . . Lady Stella!" Vega gasped as she glanced over at Piper. "Right?"

"Uh-huh." Piper nodded.

"So?" Scarlet huffed.

"No—I mean, it's Lady Stella when she was our age," Vega elaborated. "When she was just . . . *student* Stella."

That was enough to distract everyone from the task at hand, at least for the moment.

"Oooh! I want to see!" Gemma grabbed the book from Vega and studied the holo-page intently.

Even Scarlet leaned in a little closer to see the photo of two teenage girls, who were holding hands. The tall sophisticated-looking one with long golden-pink hair and a Bright Day crown on her head was almost certainly a younger version of their headmistress.

"Holy stars," exclaimed Adora, reaching over to grab the book from Gemma. "Look how super celestial that dress is! And those boots! She was so beautiful, even back then."

"She and her friend look so happy," Gemma noticed.

"C'mon, guys," Scarlet said. "Looking at old holophotos of Lady Stella won't help us figure out anything about Lady Cordial or Rancora or whatever you want to call her."

"I'm actually getting a strange feeling this staryear-book is really important," murmured Piper.

"Piper thinks this is important. Let's take a quick look," Adora urged. "Then we can go check out Lady Cordial's office. It's not like we have to be in class for a while, anyway."

"Actually, I think we should do more than take a quick look," Vega said. "As long as we're going into this old staryearbook, I might as well holo-hack into it. That way, it'll automatically link us to any important info from any other relevant holo-document, like a journal or letter."

"Wow, that's so cool, Vega," said Cassie, impressed with Vega's tech skills.

So, as the girls all gathered around, Vega tapped on the image of young Stella, and a holo-vid detailing her time at Starling Academy—long before she became headmistress—began to play before their eyes. . . .

PART ONE

A FRIEND'S BETRAYAL

1

It was a bright and sunny afternoon, and Stella couldn't stop smiling. She linked arms with her best friend, Cora, who had just gifted her with a Bright Day crown of flowers, and they ran down the grassy hill to rejoin the rest of their friends. More than a dozen classmates, most of them in their final year at Starling Academy like Stella and Cora, had gathered on the lush banks of Luminous Lake and were already enjoying the cookies and glimmerchips with star-dip that Cora had set out on fuzzy pink picnic blankets.

Stella looked over at Cora, who was wearing a knee-length party dress that perfectly complemented her long silvery-blue hair. She still couldn't get over the fact that Cora had secretly planned this whole party without her finding out. There *had* been a few moments during the last few weeks when she'd noticed Cora sneaking around their dorm room or acting a tiny bit suspicious—but any time Stella had questioned her behavior, Cora had always managed to offer a perfectly logical explanation. It was no wonder she'd played the lead roles in all of Starling Academy's theatrical productions since they were first-year students. Cora was a born performer.

"Hey! Who has a glamera?" Stella called out as she adjusted the Bright Day crown on top of her head. The pink and white flowers shimmered and released puffs of sparkling stardust with a sweetly spicy scent, and they matched the color of Stella's tailored pink minidress perfectly.

"I do!" shouted Gloria, a short girl with close-cropped green hair and thick-rimmed glasses, holding up the boxy handheld device with a pop-up screen on the top. Gloria was the head of the staryearbook committee, so she never went anywhere without her glamera and tripod.

"Oh, of course you do!" Stella laughed. "Would you mind taking some holo-movies of me with Cora?"

"Anything for the Bright Day girl!" Gloria got up from the picnic blanket and aimed the glamera in Stella and Cora's direction.

Stella smiled as she turned to face Cora and grabbed both of her hands. The best-friend charms they wore around their necks glinted in the sunlight.

"Say 'zoomberries!'" Gloria instructed.

"Zoomberries!" Stella and Cora shouted in unison as they leaned back and began to spin around in a circle—faster and faster until they began to levitate off the ground. All of the girls who were gathered down below clapped and cheered as the two best friends floated up so high that they nearly reached the treetops. As they continued to pick up speed, Stella's rosy-hued hair and dress blended with Cora's pale blue clothes and hair until they appeared to combine in a blurry, sparkling lavender ball.

"You look like you've turned into an enormous Wish Orb. You must be spinning at a minimum of three hundred revolutions per minute!" called out their math-obsessed friend Nicola in amazement.

Finally, when Stella and Cora couldn't keep up the pace any longer, they dropped down to the ground and collapsed in a fit of laughter.

"I thought my levitation skills were good, but the two of you are incredible!" Gloria said before turning to get some holo-footage of the other party guests.

Their spinning trick was pretty amazing. Cora had come up with the idea and convinced Stella to try it. It was one of the best parts of their friendship; Cora's adventurous spirit rubbed off on Stella.

"Oh, Cora!" Stella looked over at her friend as they

lay side by side on the grass. "Thank you for throwing me the best Bright Day party ever!"

"Were you really surprised?" Cora asked, widening her light blue eyes.

"I really was." Stella grinned.

"I'm so glad," Cora sighed. "I wanted to make sure it was extra special since you weren't able to go home to celebrate with your family."

Without warning, Stella's eyes began to well up with tears. As fun as the party had been, and as happy as she was to celebrate it with Cora and the rest of her friends, it was the first time she had spent a Bright Day without her parents and three younger sisters. During her previous years at Starling Academy, she had traveled home to be with them. But this year, getting a swift train ticket had been impossible because there was an energy drought, meaning more Starlings than ever before had started taking public transportation to help conserve wish energy.

"I'm sorry." Cora reached over to wipe away the glittery pink teardrop that was sliding down Stella's cheek. "I shouldn't have said that."

"Don't be sorry. I'll get to see them soon enough—when we graduate!" Stella quickly brightened and jumped to her feet, pulling Cora with her. "Come on, I want to try some of that zoomberry cake."

"Okay!" Cora agreed, following Stella over to the shiny glass picnic table, where a huge cake was decorated with bright pink letters spelling out HAPPY BRIGHT DAY, STELLA! "Who's ready for cake?" Cora called out to the rest of the party guests.

Stella's heart felt like it was going to burst with positive energy as everyone made a circle around the table and joined hands to sing to her. Then, as Cora focused her blue eyes intently on the cake, a spectacular fountain of shimmering light streamed out of the letters on top and morphed into the shape of a brilliant star. Stella's mouth dropped open as she marveled at her friend's masterful energy manipulation.

"Make a wish!" Cora urged.

Stella smiled, inhaled deeply, squeezed her eyes shut, and focused all of her energy on the same Bright Day wish she'd been making since she'd taken her first Tiny Wishology class in Wee Constellation School: *I wish I could be the greatest wish energy scientist that Starland has ever seen!* She blew on the star and it went shooting up into the sky. Then, as everyone clapped and took turns hugging Stella, Cora served the cake.

"Wow," Stella enthused as she sat down at the picnic table and took a bite. "This tastes exactly like my mother's zoomberry cake!"

"Really?" Cora's face glowed even brighter than before. "I called her to get the recipe and tested it in the lab at least four times to make sure I had it exactly right."

Stella's eyes welled up with tears again—but this time, they were from pure joy. "You're the best, Cora—thank you."

"You would do the same thing for me," Cora replied with a shrug, taking a big bite of cake. "Especially if it involved testing anything out in the lab!"

"That's true." Stella grinned and looked up at the sky, which was turning from a shimmering blue to pale pink as day turned to lightfall.

Just then, Nicola walked over from the picnic blanket where she'd been sitting with Gloria and set down her empty cake plate. "Hey, Stella," she said, brushing away a few blades of grass from her copper-colored skirt. "I hate to break up such a fantastic party but we should probably get to our meeting now, don't you think?" Stella looked down at the golden moon watch on her wrist and realized the small star was well past the five. "Oh, my stars! I almost forgot!" Stella was president of the Wishology Club, and Nicola was vice president. They had a meeting at the same time every week, but in all the Bright Day excitement, it had completely slipped Stella's mind.

"Oh, no!" Cora frowned. "I'm so sorry—I can't believe I planned your party for the same time as your meeting."

"You didn't," Stella pointed out. "We've just been having so much fun that it's gone longer than you probably expected it to."

"True," Cora said with a smile. "But I guess you'd better get going now."

"But—but I want to help you clean up," Stella stammered.

"No, it's fine." Cora shook her head and insisted that Stella go.

But Stella felt torn. She couldn't believe she was letting down the Wishology Club by running late, and now she was going to have to let down her best friend, too. It was so unlike her, forgetting a meeting—especially a Wishology Club meeting.

"Are you *positive*?" Stella asked.

"Yes!" Cora widened her pale blue eyes with a hint of impatience.

"Okay. If you're sure you don't mind," Stella said, frowning apologetically as she got up from the picnic table.

"I don't! Honestly!" Cora reached out her arms and gave Stella a reassuring hug.

"All right," Stella replied with a grateful smile. "We can finish celebrating later."

"Of course we can."

"Thank you again for the best party ever." Stella gave Cora's hand one last grateful squeeze and waved good-bye to the other guests. Then, as she linked arms with Nicola and headed off toward Halo Hall, she glanced back to give Cora a final beaming smile. She couldn't have wished for a more perfect party or for a better friend.

2

The next day, Stella stifled a yawn as she sat in Advanced Astral Accounting class. She and Cora had stayed up late celebrating her Bright Day, holo-texting with Cora's boyfriend Theodore and his best friend Ozzie, and stuffing themselves with leftover zoomberry cake. She did her best to pay attention to Professor Gibbous as he projected a series of complicated equations on the screen at the front of the classroom and excitedly explained how to solve each one. But all Stella really wanted to do was go back to bed.

"So you see, Starlings, that is the simplest way to measure the levels of positive wish energy!" Professor Gibbous concluded, rubbing his chubby hands together and bouncing in his shiny red loafers. His face turned almost as red as his sparkly beard and hair—or, at least, the small amount of fuzz that formed a halo-like band around the bald spot on top of his head.

Stella stared at the professor, then glanced down at her holo-textbook and up at the equations on the screen at the front of the classroom again. She was trying to wrap her head around all the numbers, but there didn't seem to be anything simple about them. She turned her attention to the front row, where Cora was seated, and raised the antenna on her large Star-Zap, punching in a quick holo-message asking if *she* understood what Professor Gibbous meant. She quickly added I AM SO SLEEPY! with a bleary-eyed smiley face.

Just then, the voice of their headmistress, Lady Astrid, came through the classroom speakers. "Students, please direct your attention to the front of your classrooms for an important message that is being broadcast across all of Starland!" she said as a hologram appeared at the front of the classroom. The students were surprised to see it was Andromeda Glint, president of Starland, and immediately sat up a bit taller.

"Greetings, citizens of Starland," said President Glint. She had neatly styled golden-pink hair—almost the exact same shade as Stella's—that formed a big pouf around her head, and she wore a suit with a large sparkly silver star pinned to her lapel. "My sincerest apologies for the intrusion, but I'm coming to you today with an important announcement. As you all know, Starland is facing a positive energy drought—and although we have assembled a team of top wish energy scientists who are working hard to find a solution, the conservation and recycling efforts that were recently put into effect have become more of a priority than ever before."

A few of Stella's classmates began to chatter softly to each other, but Professor Gibbous quickly silenced them by sliding his glasses down his nose and raising his bushy red eyebrows—his standard firm-but-friendly warning for them to quiet down.

"I know that these efforts haven't been easy for anyone and I thank you for the sacrifices you've already made," President Glint continued. "It is my hope that you will continue to do everything you can, as well as come up with additional solutions to help ensure that we maintain the precious positive energy resources that are so vital to keeping our world running."

As the president kept talking, the screen of Stella's Star-Zap lit up with a holo-text from Cora: DIDN'T THEO LOOK SO CUTE LAST NIGHT? ☺ The screen went dark and then lit up again with another holo-text: OH, AND I'M SOOO TIRED. GIBBOUS IS MAKING NO SENSE TO ME. AS USUAL! Cora ended the note with her usual sign-off—an image of her taking a bow. But this time, after doing so, the image fell down and went to sleep.

HA! Stella holo-texted back before lowering the antenna and closing her Star-Zap so she could listen to the rest of the president's message.

"Many of you will be receiving additional instructions and requests from local officials, school administrators, and the like, and I urge you to give those directives your immediate attention," President Glint said. "Of course, your government is here to support you in any way we can, but all Starlings must work together to make sure that we address this challenge. So long as we all remain committed to retaining our positive energy levels, I know we can get it done. Thank you and good day."

As the holographic image faded away, the voice of Lady Astrid came through the loudspeaker again. "Students, as President Glint said, some local officials— including school administrators—have received additional instructions regarding the drought," the headmistress began. "Specifically, because you are some of the best and brightest students on all of Starland, the president herself has proposed that this year's annual Starling Academy Wish-Science Fair projects should focus on ways to solve the positive energy drought—above and beyond the conservation and recycling efforts already in place."

As president of the Wishology Club, Stella was stunned. The club had been discussing the Wish-Science

Fair at their meeting the previous day—and normally they were the ones who proposed the theme to Lady Astrid each year. Why hadn't she called them in to discuss all of this first?

"But that isn't all," Lady Astrid continued. "Upon graduation, the winner of this year's fair will be offered a most coveted position working for Starland's prestigious Wish-Tank!"

At that, the entire class erupted into excited chatter, and Stella was no longer annoyed that the Wishology Club hadn't been consulted about the fair—nor was she sleepy anymore. Starlings who worked in the Wish-Tank were responsible for granting some of Wishworld's most challenging and important wishes! Stella had always dreamed of going to work there after graduation, but even with her near-perfect grades and academic achievements, she couldn't be certain that she would be granted a spot in the Wish-Tank. They only took two graduating students from all of Starland each year! And now one of those spots was guaranteed to a Starling Academy student! She was determined it would be her.

When Lady Astrid wrapped up her announcement, Professor Gibbous began pacing in front of the classroom, then stopped abruptly and turned to look at his students, raising his sparkly red eyebrows at them.

"Well, this all applies very nicely to today's lesson,

don't you think?" he asked, clasping his hands together expectantly as some of the students nodded in response. "So, tell me . . . do any of you have any theories about the reasons for the current drought—and why we must all work so diligently to conserve and recycle Starland's positive energy?"

Before Stella could raise her hand, Nicola—who was sitting front and center—beat her to the punch and the professor called on her.

"In my Wish Fulfillment class, we've been talking about the fact that Wishling girls have always made the purest and most powerful wishes of all—but they haven't been making nearly enough of them lately," Nicola said, tucking a lock of her short bronze-colored hair behind one of her ears. "I think maybe that's why there's been less positive wish energy available on Starland—and that's why we need to be careful about how much we use."

"Indeed." Professor Gibbous nodded approvingly. "That is an excellent theory! Starland scientists do believe that Wishworld's current decade has been particularly challenging for girls *and* women. But, as the president said, it's up to all of us to work together to come up with creative solutions to this drought—and, as Lady Astrid said, this will be the basis of your Wish-Science Fair projects this year, should you choose to enter. With such a coveted and prestigious award being offered, I have no doubt you will put in an unprecedented amount of effort!"

Stella felt a bit lightheaded as she began to process all of this new information. She had already been working on a few different drought-related ideas with the Wishology Club—mostly finding ways to reduce, reuse, and recycle positive wish energy—but what Nicola had said about girls on Wishworld making fewer wishes was sparking some new ideas as well. Stella's head was becoming positively flooded with thoughts about helping girls on Wishworld *and* winning the Wish-Science Fair.

Most of all, she was already picturing herself dressed in a shiny silver lab coat, walking toward the Starland Wish-Tank offices and placing her hand on the scanner that permitted only a select few access inside. Was it a real possibility for her, though? She could hardly wait to find out!

3

"Can you believe it?" Stella asked Cora as they exited their Astral Accounting class and headed to the Celestial Café for lunch. "A job in the Wish-Tank for winning the Wish-Science Fair!"

Cora couldn't help smiling at her friend's extreme enthusiasm. "So I guess you're not sleepy anymore?"

"I don't know that I'll ever be sleepy again!" Stella said, her face growing brighter with each step she took. "There's not going to be any *time* to sleep! I'm going to need to spend every available moment coming up with the best possible solution to the drought. I *have* to win the Wish-Science Fair, Cora. I just have to!"

"It *is* pretty incredible—the exact job you've always wanted," Cora replied. "And there's no way anyone *but* you is going to win."

"You've taken first place every year!"

"True—but you heard what Professor Gibbous said, right? With a prize like that, everybody's going to try extra hard to win." Stella sighed and was about to open the door to the Celestial Café when a Bad Wish Orb suddenly zoomed overhead.

"Yikes!" Stella ducked as the dark sphere, crackling with negative energy and surrounded by a terrifying purple aura, zipped by her. "That almost hit us!"

"Yeah." Cora shook her head as she watched the orb go flying off in the direction of the Negative Energy Facility, leaving a trail of gray fog in its wake. "I've never seen one that close before."

Although Cora was only temporarily thrown off by the ball of negative energy, she could see Stella was still shivering in her glittery pink dress as they headed for their usual table on the far end of the café. It was right next to a window, where they could look out and see Luminous Lake.

"May I take your order?" asked a silver four-wheeled Bot-Bot waiter as it rolled up to Stella. It had a long cylindrical body with a domed head, and it held a silver tray in one of its pincerlike hands.

"Um." Stella blinked at the waiter dizzily, her face paler than Cora had ever seen it.

"Hey—are you okay?" Cora asked her friend.

"I—I don't know," Stella replied. "I'm still thinking about that Bad Wish Orb. I wonder if it infected me with its negative energy! I've completely lost my appetite."

"Oh, my stars, Stella—I'm sure it didn't infect you." Cora tried to offer her friend a reassuring smile.

"I think I'll just have a cup of Zing," Stella told the waiter.

As the Bot-Bot waited patiently for Cora's order, Cora and Stella looked up to see their classmate Devorah stopping at their table—so abruptly that her two best friends, Delia and Diana, nearly crashed into her. All three girls had long platinum hair and matching glittery headbands—pale blue for Devorah, lavender for Delia, and pink for Diana. Because they had developed a reputation for being kind of mean and self-absorbed, a lot of their classmates referred to them as The Killer Ds. However, they'd always been nice to Cora, and she found them more entertaining than evil.

"Hey, Devorah," Cora said with a smile. "Do you guys want to join us?"

"Sure!" Devorah immediately dropped into the chair next to Cora and motioned for Delia and Diana to sit by Stella before launching into a tirade about the energy drought. "Is it just me, or are these energy restrictions crazy? I mean, have you ever seen my hair look so dull? I feel like a complete Wishling! But how can I get it to shine when our sparkle showers turn off after three minutes? It's maddening!"

"Oh, please." Cora shook her head. "Your hair always looks shinier than anyone else's. I'm super jealous."

"You're just saying that," Devorah replied, all wide-eyed false modesty.

"I'm not!" Cora insisted. "It almost makes me want to find a way around that rule, too."

But Devorah looked skeptical. After all, she knew what a good actress Cora was. Not only had they gotten to know each other pretty well in Practice Wish Orb Mastery class, where Cora had impressed everyone with her ability to look and sound exactly like a real Wishling, but Devorah was also in the Drama Club with Cora. She wasn't particularly good at acting, but she had convinced the rest of the club to let her join because her mother was a famous Starland actress. It was Cora's dream to be as famous as Devorah's mom one day.

"May I take your order?" repeated the Bot-Bot waiter, who had remained patiently by Stella's side. He swiveled his silver head around and directed his blinking red eyes at Devorah.

"I'll just have a garble green salad," Devorah replied. "Otherwise I'm going to blow up like a cocomoon."

"Me too," echoed Delia and Diana in unison.

"I think I'll have mushmoon and moonion casserole with a side of glimmerchips, please," Cora said before turning to look at Stella. "You really need to eat something, too, you know," she told her friend, in the exact same way her mother used to instruct her to eat at every meal, whether she was hungry or not.

"Oh, all right." Stella sighed, looking up at the waiter. "May I have a small serving of mushmoon and moonion casserole, too, please?"

"Right away," the Bot-Bot waiter replied, and then rolled away.

"That's the spirit!" Cora grinned at Stella and then shifted her focus back to Devorah. "So—back to the drought. I honestly don't think we're going to need to worry about it much longer."

"Really?" Devorah's blue eyes sparkled hopefully. "Why not?"

"Because Stella's going to put an end to it as soon as she figures out her Wish-Science Fair project."

"Oh!" Devorah clapped her hands and leaned across the table, gazing at Stella gratefully. "That would be *brilliant*. Daddy gave me a brand-new Starcar for my Bright Day last month and I haven't been able to use it because we all have to take the swift train now." Devorah rolled her eyes. "It's so dim, don't you think?"

Delia and Diana nodded their dutiful support while Cora and Stella discreetly exchanged amused smiles.

"So how are you going to end it?" Devorah asked.

"I'm not sure yet," Stella replied, frowning. "But I keep thinking about what Nicola said in our Astral Accounting class—that the drought might be due to Wishling girls not making enough wishes."

"We've been talking about that in my Advanced Wish Fulfillment class, too." Devorah shook her head in frustration. "But it seems strange that girls wouldn't be making tons of wishes. I mean, how could anyone run out of things to want?"

"I'm beginning to think it has something to do with what Professor Gibbous said—that it's difficult for girls and women on Wishworld right now," Stella replied.

"Really?" Devorah asked. "What's so difficult about it?"

"Well, for one thing, we know girls aren't given as many opportunities as boys," Stella noted. "A lot of Wishling girls are told that they shouldn't even bother going to college—and some colleges don't even accept girls."

"It's true," Cora said, thinking back to some of the simulated trips she'd taken to Wishworld in Practice Wish Orb Mastery class. "A lot of the Wishling girls I've seen are told that they should focus on getting married instead of going to college or getting jobs—and then they're expected to do all the cooking and cleaning, and their husbands give them an *allowance* and tell them how to dress, where they can go, what they can do."

"Wow!" Devorah gasped. "They're practically treated like pet glowfurs!"

"It's awful." Stella frowned. "Some places even have policies against hiring Wishling women—and if they do go to work, they're paid less than Wishling men doing the same exact thing."

"And we know that hardly any women hold positions of power, like in the government," Cora added. "Plus, Wishlings with darker skin have to go to different schools than the ones with lighter skin—and in some places, they're not allowed to drink from the same sparkler fountains or go to the same places to eat."

"I just don't get it," Devorah commented with a look of horror in her pale blue eyes. "We wouldn't even be eating at the same lunch table right now! The reds and the pinks, the yellows and the greens, the purples and the blues—everyone would have to be kept apart. How silly!"

"And how sad," Cora added with a frown as she imagined what it would be like to be forced to go to a different school from Stella, simply because of their colors—and how dull Starling Academy would look if everyone were the same color.

"No wonder they're not making enough wishes," Stella said glumly. "They've probably given up hope. They're discouraged."

Seeing how sad her friend was becoming, Cora felt compelled to steer the conversation in a more positive direction. "At least we get to live on Starland, where girls and boys all have the same opportunities and we don't have to live by some arbitrary color-coded set of rules," she pointed out. Then, thinking more about how easy it would be to solve the problem, she added, "If I went down to Wishworld, I would show girls and Wishlings of all colors that they can do anything they set their stars on—that they just have to believe in themselves."

"Oh, Cora—you've just given me the best idea!" Stella gasped, jumping up from the table so quickly that she nearly knocked over the Bot-Bot waiter, who was returning with the girls' orders. "Oh, my stars. Oh, my stars!"

Then, before Cora or anyone else could stop her, Stella had raced right out of the Celestial Café.

"Your friend is a little crazy, huh?" Devorah smirked at Cora as she placed her sparkly silver napkin on her lap.

"Yeah, but that's just part of her charm," Cora replied

with a laugh. "She's kind of like a mad scientist—which is why I'm sure she's going to put an end to this drought and win the Wish-Science Fair."

"I hope you're right." Devorah sighed and took a bite of lighttuce.

"I know I am," Cora replied, digging into her casserole.

In fact, she had never been more certain of anything in her life.

Stella hurried along the Cosmic Transporter, nearly bumping into a few of her fellow students as she raced from the Celestial Café toward Halo Hall. In her haste, she was thrown almost completely off balance when her Star-Zap began buzzing and she looked down to see a holo-text from Cora:

WHAT'S GOING ON? WHY DID YOU LEAVE WITHOUT EAT-ING LUNCH?

Stella was so eager to get to class, she didn't want to take time to pause for a reply—but she knew she owed Cora some sort of explanation. So she quickly replied:

SORRY! I'LL TELL YOU WHEN YOU GET TO CLASS!

Almost instantly, another text came through:

BUT YOU DIDN'T HAVE ANYTHING TO EAT!

Stella rolled her eyes impatiently, but she also had to smile at her friend's concern. In all the years they had spent together at Starling Academy, Cora had become like a sister to her—and when she was being particularly protective, like now, a second mother. So she sent another quick reply:

I KNOW. I'LL EAT LATER. PLEASE DON'T WORRY. :) BUT ALSO, THANK YOU FOR WORRYING. ;) SEE YOU SOON!

As Stella lowered the antenna on her Star-Zap and entered the classroom, Professor Shannon looked up from her desk. Her emerald hair framed her round face in short waves and was clipped over her ear on one side with a beautiful star-shaped pin made from dazzling white gemstones. It was the perfect complement to her shiny green dress, with its sparkly little star-shaped buttons down the front.

"You're here early," the professor said, giving Stella a warm smile. "And without Cora? I don't think I've ever seen the two of you apart!"

"I know—it doesn't happen too often," Stella replied with a grin, "but I couldn't wait to get here."

"Well, I certainly appreciate your enthusiasm." Professor Shannon's green eyes twinkled as she nodded approvingly at Stella. "But is there a special reason for today's eagerness?"

"Yes—I was talking with Cora and some other friends about possible reasons for the drought and all sorts of ways to solve it," Stella told the instructor as she took a seat in the front row. "So I wanted to start recording some holo-notes right away, and I was wondering if we might even be able to discuss the drought in class today."

"Hmmm." The professor drummed her fingers on her desk and tilted her head, contemplating the suggestion while Stella powered up her holo-notebook. "That's an interesting suggestion."

The Wishworld Relations instructor regularly encouraged her students to come in with ideas for timely topics that the class could discuss—and when she felt the idea was strong enough, she would even let the student who had proposed it take over as the lecturer for the day. Stella was almost certain—or at least hopeful—that she was about to be placed in that esteemed position. Her stomach fluttered with nervous excitement as she began recording some holo-notes and more students began filing in, their voices energizing the room as they chatted with each other and made their way toward their seats.

"Hi," said Stella's classmate Indirra as she sat down to Stella's right. She had big lavender eyes and her purple hair was tied back in a single braid that hung halfway down her back. "Exciting announcement about the Wish-Science Fair earlier, don't you think?"

Stella wasn't quite sure how to respond. Indirra was in the Wishology Club with Stella, and she also happened to be one of the fiercest competitors in the Wish-Science

Fair, having come in second place—right behind Stella—every staryear. There were never any hard feelings as far as Stella could tell, but it did make her wonder if she should really present any of her preliminary ideas about the drought during class after all. Even though the ultimate goal was to help Starland, she didn't want to give away anything that might ruin her chances of taking first place—and of going to work in the Starland Wish-Tank! As soon as the thought of that incredible prize entered her head, Stella felt like a swarm of flutterfocuses were dancing in her stomach again.

"*Beyond* exciting," Stella finally agreed with a nod.

But Indirra had already shifted her attention to the holo-notebook on her desk. She wasn't being rude, though. Stella knew that Indirra was simply incredibly driven when it came to school, and she didn't spend a lot of time making conversation unless there was a clear purpose for it. So Stella returned her attention to her own holo-notes, becoming so absorbed with one idea in particular that she was completely startled when Cora arrived and tapped her on the shoulder.

"Um—hellooo?" Cora seemed a bit irritated as she settled into the seat to Stella's left.

"Hi!" Stella beamed at her friend, eager to explain why she'd left the café so suddenly by showing her some of the ideas she'd already come up with for her

Wish-Science Fair project. But before she had a chance to reveal a single holo-note, Professor Shannon got up from her desk and addressed the class.

"All right, everyone, please quiet down," the instructor said as the last few students filed in and took their seats. "I had been planning a lecture on Wishling communication skills for today—but Stella had a wonderful idea for another topic that I think we should explore instead."

Stella felt her cheeks begin to glow when the professor mentioned her name and smiled kindly in her direction. She glanced over at Cora with a grin and then looked down at her extensive holo-notes. Once again, she wondered if she should share anything that might put her at a disadvantage in the Wish-Science Fair. But there was no turning back now, as all eyes in the classroom were already on her—and the more she thought about it, the more she realized that if she didn't share her ideas openly, she would be in violation of several of Starling Academy's Five Points of a Star Student:

Think carefully, creatively, and courageously.
Act in the best interests of all Starlings.
Follow your own unique path.
Give more than you receive.
Be a shining light for others.

"Stella, would you like to tell the class what you wanted to discuss today?" Professor Shannon added.

"Sure." Stella nodded and cleared her throat. "After the announcement earlier today about the theme for this year's Wish-Science Fair, I thought it might be good for us to talk about the drought."

Almost immediately, Stella could feel a strange energy coming from either side of her, as both Indirra and Cora raised their hands.

"Yes, Indirra?" Professor Shannon called on her first.

"I'm sorry, but I don't see how the drought has anything to do with Wishworld relations," Indirra replied.

"That's an interesting comment," Professor Shannon acknowledged. "Stella, how would you connect the drought to Wishworld Relations?"

"Well," Stella said, glancing down at her holo-notes for a moment before sitting up a bit taller in her chair, "when we talk about Wishworld Relations, we often think about how Starlings should be interacting with Wishlings—but we should also be thinking about how *Wishlings* interact with each other, and especially how all of these relationships affect what they believe about themselves."

Stella looked up at the professor, who was narrowing her eyes and slowly nodding. "I think I see where you're going—but please continue."

"Right now on Wishworld, a lot of girls aren't given as many opportunities as boys—they're essentially given the message that they aren't capable of the same things," Stella noted, repeating what she'd mentioned earlier at the café. "This may explain why Wishling girls aren't making as many wishes—because they don't believe that anything is possible—and that may be why there's less positive energy available on Starland."

"Ahhh," the instructor said with an enthusiastic nod, and several of Stella's classmates—including Indirra—responded in a similarly enlightened way as they began to understand the connection she was making. "That is a most promising theory. Can you give us an example?"

"Yes . . ." Stella paused for a moment and searched through her holo-notes for one of the ideas she'd come up with after what Cora had said at the café. "Maybe there was a young Wishling girl who loved playing star ball when she was little, but as she got older, she discovered that there weren't any professional star ball teams for girls—there were only teams for boys. So she stopped playing."

Stella looked up at Professor Shannon, who nodded sadly. "Yes, our observations suggest that there are many star ball teams—or what Wishlings call basketball teams—for boys, but not as many for girls," she confirmed. "The same is true for many other athletic endeavors on Wishworld. We don't see nearly as many girls competing as boys, largely because they're told they can't or they shouldn't. So how might this affect the number of wishes being made?"

"It's like I was saying before, when girls aren't given the same opportunities as boys, their idea of what's possible is limited," Stella replied, her eyes beginning to burn with tears at the mere thought of it. "When that happens, they might stop wishing for the things they really want. They might stop trying. They might not even *think* about trying."

As Stella's voice trailed off, Cora raised her hand and Professor Shannon called on her.

"The same sort of thing might be happening with Wishlings who have darker skin," Cora pointed out, repeating what she had said at the Celestial Café earlier. "They're not given as many opportunities as Wishlings with lighter skin, and they're told they're not good enough to go to the same schools or eat at the same places, so maybe they aren't making as many big wishes as they should be, either."

As Cora spoke, Stella heard someone giggling in the back of the room and turned to see who would laugh at something so awful.

"Gail! Dawn! What do you find so amusing back

there?" Professor Shannon snapped, echoing Stella's thoughts.

"It makes no sense," said Dawn, whose short, stubby red pigtails were practically perpendicular to either side of her head. She was the captain of the Glowin' Glions, Starling Academy's top-ranked star ball team. "Why wouldn't there be just as many sports teams for Wishling girls as boys—and how could they *possibly* decide that one color is better than another?"

"Yeah—everyone knows that girls and boys are equal and so are all the colors," Gail agreed, rolling her dark cobalt eyes before adding with a smirk, "although I guess blue girls *might* be better at sports!"

"Ah." Professor Shannon's face softened into a gentle smile again. "It does seem strange, doesn't it? But as Stella and Cora have so wisely pointed out, the circumstances on Wishworld are different from those on Starland. Many Wishlings are still learning things that we already know."

"That's horrible," Dawn fumed angrily, her rosy cheeks turning nearly as red as her hair.

"Isn't it just?" Professor Shannon's green lips turned down in an exaggerated frown. "But assuming that what Stella and Cora are saying is true, what could we do about it, in terms of Wishworld Relations—and how might that affect the flow of positive wish energy to Starland?"

Stella was about to reply—but before she could, Cora raised her hand and the professor called on her.

"If I were a Wish-Granter, I would try to lead by example," Cora said, twirling a lock of pale blue hair around her finger. "So, for instance, if Wishling girls were told that they couldn't take a particular class because it's only for boys—like Starcar mechanics or wood shop—I would march right in, disguised as a Wishling girl, of course, and show them that I *can* take those classes and do every bit as well as any Wishling boy. Then Wishling girls would be filled with hope again and motivated to make more wishes."

"Wonderful!" The professor's eyes sparkled happily as she looked from Cora to Stella, who smiled over at her friend and raised her hand, eager to add a few more of her own thoughts to the conversation.

"Yes, Stella?" Professor Shannon nodded.

"May I demonstrate?" Stella asked.

"Certainly." The professor smoothed down her green dress and motioned for Stella to come to the front of the classroom. "Please take over."

"Okay!" Stella felt her stomach flutter with nervous excitement as she carefully stepped over Cora and the other students in her row and headed to the front of the classroom.

"So, we assume that girls on Wishworld have been told that they can't do the same things as boys," Stella began, punching a few keys on her holo-notepad so an image of a sad Wishling girl floated up into the air, with a group of happy and victorious boys behind her.

"*But* there are some girls who are making big wishes—which means they haven't given up hope." Again, Stella punched a few keys and another image of a Wishling girl appeared, this one smiling with hands stretched over her head victoriously. She tapped on the image and a Wish Orb floated up and away from the smiling girl. "So, I would propose that when Wish-Granters go on Wish Missions, they should not only focus on the primary Wisher—as important as that is—but also use any extra time they have available to interact with other Wishlings who may have stopped believing in themselves, so they can show them that they're capable of a lot more than they might realize."

"Very nice," Professor Shannon noted, looking from Stella to Cora. "And this would be accomplished when the Wish-Granter leads by example—showing other Wishlings how to stand up for and believe in themselves?"

"That's one possibility," Stella agreed, scanning through her holo-notes, "but it's not the only option."

"Please explain," the professor said.

"Well, let's say that the primary mission has to do with helping a Wishling girl get what she wants—anything she wants, really, like a good grade on a test or an invitation to a special party," Stella began, referring to the image of the happy, victorious girl who had made a big wish. "While there, the Wish-Granter could pay close attention to the things that the primary Wisher's *friends* are good at, too—like the example of the girl who loved star ball, but discovered there wasn't a team for girls."

Stella punched a few more keys and an image of a girl floated up next to the one in the victory pose—but this girl was holding a star ball, and she was staring at it intently, as if contemplating whether or not she should continue to hold on to it. The girl was frowning, and appeared to have given up hope.

"In this situation, the Wish-Granter *could* start a star ball team and invite the girl to join—leading by example, as Cora said—*or* the Wish-Granter could simply remind the girl of how talented she is and encourage her to start a team herself," Stella noted, touching another key on her holo-notepad so a group of girls in all sizes and colors gathered around the girl with the star ball. "At that point, the girl might finally wish for something that seemed out of reach before—and when her wish comes true, other girls might be motivated to make wishes, too. So it could have a ripple effect. Each Wish Mission could result in one wish granted, plus several more wishes made—so the problem of girls not making enough wishes is solved!"

Stella tapped another key and suddenly Wish Orbs began floating above all the other Wishling girls. It was quite magnificent—and when she looked up from her holo-notes, she realized that her classmates were completely spellbound as well, captivated by the images of so many new Wish Orbs. Then, as Professor Shannon nodded her approval, several of the students began to applaud—including Dawn, Gail, and even Indirra—and within a few moments, almost everyone was cheering!

Stella had presented good ideas before, but getting everyone to clap? That was a first, and it was completely thrilling! Now she finally understood what Cora meant when she talked about how fun it was to perform for live audiences. "The immediate positive feedback motivates me to do my best," Cora had explained. It all made sense now. Stella looked at Cora, excited to share the moment with her. After all, the applause was really for both of them. But Cora was completely focused on the holo-notebook on her desk and seemed oblivious to the enthusiastic response from their classmates.

"My goodness," Professor Shannon said after the applause had died down. "I think you've got some very promising theories here—and what a wonderfully creative use of Wishworld Relations to potentially solve the drought!"

"Thank you," Stella replied with a grateful smile, practically floating on a cloud of positive energy as she headed back to her seat. When she got there, she reached out to grab Cora's hand, but Cora immediately moved it away and focused on her holo-notebook. What was going on? Stella desperately wanted to talk to her, but the professor was addressing both of them now.

"In fact, Stella, I think you should really explore these ideas in depth—perhaps test them out inside a few practice Wish Orbs," Professor Shannon proposed. "If you can find a way to prove that your theories will work on Wishworld, especially among young Wishling girls, you might just have a winning project for this year's Wish-Science Fair!"

Stella lit up as she considered the professor's words. It was precisely the sort of feedback she'd been hoping for, and her head was already filling with all the possibilities: What if Wish-Granters really could help Wishlings believe in themselves again? What if young Wishling girls really did start to make more wishes, and those wishes not only came true but produced enough positive wish energy to put an end to Starland's drought? It would definitely require extensive research inside practice Wish Orbs. Maybe she and Cora could do the experiments together? They had always wanted to see each other disguised as Wishlings but had never had the chance, because they were in different Practice Wish Orb Mastery classes. Of course! It would be so much fun—and Professor Shannon even thought it might result in a winning project!

Stella thanked the instructor again. She was so glad she had decided to present her ideas, and that Cora had shared hers as well. She couldn't wait to talk with her best friend; maybe they would even do research together. But when the bell signaling the end of class rang and Stella turned to finally start chatting with Cora, she discovered that her friend's seat had already been vacated. In fact, Cora was already racing out of the classroom. She hadn't even waited for Stella!

5

Since Stella and Cora had a free period in their schedules after Wishworld Relations class, they usually went to the Lightning Lounge to get a cup of Zing together. But on that particular afternoon, it appeared that Cora would rather go by herself.

"Cora! Wait!" Stella called after her best friend, who was almost out of earshot and speeding away on the Cosmic Transporter. But instead of looking back or acknowledging Stella, Cora picked up her pace. Determined to find out what was going on, Stella mustered all the positive energy she could and finally caught up to Cora right before she got to the door of the Lightning Lounge.

"Hey!" Stella gasped, grabbing Cora by the arm.

"Ouch!" Cora winced and glared at Stella.

"Oh—sorry!" Stella frowned with genuine remorse. "Are you okay? I didn't mean to hurt you."

"Yeah, I'm fine," Cora replied tersely.

"Why were you running away from me?" Stella demanded without skipping a beat. "Why wouldn't you talk to me in class? What is going on?"

"You think you're the only one who can run off without an explanation?" Cora retorted, and, once again, turned away from Stella and headed through the sliding glass doors into the lounge.

So that was it? Cora was trying to show Stella how it had felt when she'd rushed off earlier?

"I only ran out of the café because I wanted to work on my ideas for solving the drought," Stella insisted as she followed Cora through the lounge past small groups of students—some sipping Zing, others reading holo-books or playing games of cosmic cards.

But Cora still wouldn't stop, and within a few moments she had arrived at their favorite spot in the corner, directly beneath a large rooftop window that allowed the maximum amount of light to stream in.

"*Your* ideas?" Cora scoffed, dropping into her usual bright blue chair while Stella sat down in the plush pink one opposite it. Continuing to avoiding Stella's gaze, Cora waved her index finger at a holo-zine that was lying on a small silver table between them, prompting it to float into her hands.

"Well, yes." Stella nodded, wrinkling up her nose. "The ideas that I presented in class—the ones I came up with after what you said in the café."

"Right." Cora finally looked up from her holo-zine, her blue eyes clouding over with an anger Stella had never seen before. "So not *exactly* your ideas."

A knot began forming in Stella's stomach as she considered Cora's words. "Oh—it was definitely thanks to what you had said in the café," Stella acknowledged. "I mean, of course I owe you some of the credit! That's why I said you'd given me the best idea before I left— and I was thinking we should work together. Because we *both* had such good ideas!"

"So I should just help you, so you can win the Wish-Science Fair and take all the credit?" Cora's blue lips began to tremble.

"Well, it's not like *you* are going to enter the contest," Stella replied. She was confused. Cora had never even tried to enter the Wish-Science Fair before. She was busy being the lead in almost every one of the school's theater productions; Cora's dream was to be an actor.

Cora looked up from her holo-zine again, her eyes darker than ever. "Well, what if I *did* want to enter the

Wish-Science Fair? Is it so hard to believe that I might be able to? That I might even win?"

"Oh." Stella clutched the arms of her chair tightly as she realized Cora might actually be serious.

"Don't you think I could do it?" Cora asked. "Prove that *my* idea would work, I mean."

"Of course I do," Stella insisted. "But it would require a lot of research—and putting together a whole project for the Wish-Science Fair isn't as easy as it might look."

"Ha!" Cora laughed scornfully. "It does look pretty easy when you steal your best friend's ideas and pass them off as your own!"

Stella gasped. How could Cora think something so awful? She would *never* try to pass off someone else's ideas as her own—and her ideas were different enough from Cora's. Weren't they? Stella's thoughts flashed back to everything they'd discussed in class, all the examples she'd given. Everything she'd presented had been her own, from *her* holo-notebook—not Cora's! Yes, Stella did say that Cora had given her the idea when she raced out of the café. But she'd already acknowledged that much—and besides, everything she'd come up with after that was hers. Wasn't it?

"You're wrong, Cora," Stella finally replied softly, tears beginning to well up in her eyes. "You know I would never steal anything from you."

"Really?" said Cora, getting up from her chair and staring at the holo-zine in her hands, sending it zooming back onto the silver table with a clatter so loud that it startled some of their nearby classmates. "Because it feels like maybe there's a lot about you that I don't know."

Then, before Stella could respond, Cora was storming out of the Lightning Lounge without looking back. It was the second time she'd deserted Stella—and now that Stella understood why, it hurt twice as much.

6

As Cora reclined on the long velvety blue couch on her side of the dorm room, she adjusted the oversized cushions all around her and burrowed under the soft pale blue blanket she'd brought from her bed. After tossing and turning for most of the night, she had decided to try sleeping on the sofa. But even though she'd always found it to be even more comfortable and calming than her bed, she simply couldn't relax, let alone get any sleep. She peered over the back of the couch, stealing a glance up the spiral staircase on the other side of the room, which led to the loft where Stella's bed was located. There was no way Stella had been able to sleep that night, either—was there?

It was the first time the two best friends had ever gone to bed angry—and thinking about everything she'd said to Stella the previous afternoon made Cora's heart hurt. She snuggled against the cushions and squeezed her eyes shut, but it was still no use. As she began to push off the blanket to get up, she heard Stella tiptoeing down the stairs—so she instantly curled up into a ball and pretended to be asleep. But even with her eyes closed, Cora could sense Stella coming closer.

"Hi," she heard Stella whisper. "Are you awake?"

Cora waited a few moments and then slowly opened her eyes, rolling away from the back of the couch and glancing around the room wearily to give off the impression that she'd just awoken from the best night's sleep ever. She allowed her eyes to settle on Stella, in her cushy pink robe and slippers, her rosy-gold hair messy from sleep. "Oh. Hi."

Stella immediately sat down on the couch next to Cora and sunk into the cushions. "I'm so sorry about yesterday!" she blurted out, looking sadly into Cora's eyes.

"Me too!" Cora instantly replied, unable to keep up the nonchalant act as she reached out to give her best friend a hug. "I couldn't sleep at all, could you?"

"No." Stella shook her head, which was still buried in Cora's shoulder as they embraced. After they broke apart, Stella wiped away a few tears and frowned. "The more I thought about you saying that I'd stolen your ideas, the worse I felt."

"And the more I thought about *accusing* you of

stealing my ideas, the worse *I* felt!" Cora replied with a nervous laugh, staring down at the bright blue star-shaped rugs scattered around the gleaming silvery-blue tiled floor. "I know you would never do something like that."

"But I can see why you would feel that way," Stella acknowledged. "And honestly, if you want to enter the Wish-Science Fair with your idea, I can come up with something else."

"No!" Cora knew how important the Wish-Science Fair—and getting to work in the Wish-Tank—was to Stella. Cora had just wanted to share in some of the glory Stella had received in class the previous day—but after thinking about it, she knew she was being silly and, well, a bit melodramatic.

"Yes," Stella replied firmly. "I shouldn't have taken your idea and run so far with it like that—and you should have been up there at the front of the class, presenting it all with me. I've just been so excited ever since we found out that the winner will get a job in the Wish-Tank!"

"That's exactly why *you* need to be the one to do the research and turn it into the winning project for the Wish-Science Fair," Cora said, grabbing Stella's hand. "It's your destiny, not mine. I want you to win, and I want you to get that job."

"Really?" Stella asked.

"Really!" Cora assured her.

Stella took a few deep breaths as she let go of Cora's hand. She got up off the couch and began pacing around the room in her usual methodical way, stepping from one little rug to the next until she'd touched all of them. Then she turned around and did the same thing in the opposite direction. Finally, she stopped in her tracks and locked eyes with Cora again.

"Thank you," Stella said, her eyes shining with adoration for her friend. "But I still hope you might want to do some of the research together, and more than anything, I hope I can prove that my—I mean *our*—ideas will work."

Cora rolled her eyes and laughed kindly. "You most definitely can!"

"But I'm—or we're—going to have to test it out in a practice Wish Orb," Stella said. "In fact, we're probably going to have to test it out in tons of practice orbs before I figure out the best approach."

"If it takes that many, so be it. I know you'll find a way," Cora insisted.

"I guess. . . ." Stella nodded, lost in thought for a few moments before her entire face lit up. "You know what's going to be incredible, though?"

"What?"

"Getting to test it out on the *real* Wishworld one day!" Stella replied.

Cora had to agree. She could almost picture her friend on her very first Wish Mission, encouraging Wishlings everywhere to start believing in themselves again. The more she thought about it, the more a wish of her own began to form—that she could somehow see Stella in action, not just in a practice Wish Orb but helping *real* Wishlings—and that was when the most wonderful idea dawned on her.

"Oh, my stars, Stella!" Cora gasped, jumping up from the couch. "I know exactly what we need to do!"

"What?" Stella smiled with anticipation.

"Test out our ideas on the real Wishworld right away!"

"Huh?" Stella wrinkled up her nose, like she'd just wandered into a patch of stinkberries. "How could we possibly do *that*?"

A giant mischievous grin spread across Cora's face. "It might sound crazy, but . . . what if we snuck down there? Together!"

Stella's eyes widened in shock. She spun around and walked over to sit down on the pink stool at her vanity table, as if she needed to get as far away from the idea as possible. "Cora. You can't be serious."

But Cora had never been *more* serious. As the idea of going to Wishworld with Stella grew bigger and brighter in her mind, it was impossible to contain her excitement. "Come on! You know you've thought about it!"

Stella held up her hands and shook her head. "Not really."

"Not even a little bit?" Cora raised her pale blue eyebrows.

But instead of answering, Stella turned away and stared into her gold-framed vanity mirror. "Well, okay—yes," she finally admitted, brushing her long hair and pulling it back into a ponytail before swiveling around to face Cora again. "I have thought about it. But going to Wishworld is strictly forbidden for anyone but Wish-Granters. We won't officially be Wish-Granters until we graduate. We would get into serious trouble if anyone ever found out."

"Who would find out?" Cora asked, grabbing her blanket off the couch and wrapping it around her like a cape as she marched over to sit down on her bed. "Besides, we're practically already Starling Academy graduates—and testing out those ideas on *real* Wishlings? It's almost too perfect!"

Stella sighed and shook her head—but even as she did so, she stood up and walked over to Cora and plopped down next to her. *Yes!* Cora could tell that her friend was beginning to warm to the idea.

"The thing is . . ." Stella began slowly, and Cora could practically see her sorting out all the steps in her head as each one occurred to her, "if we did go down . . . and we tested out our theories . . . and even if we proved they would work . . . beyond any glimmer of a doubt . . . it's not like I could use any of the evidence in my Wish-Science Fair project . . . not if I gathered it illegally!"

"But at least you'd know for sure if they worked," Cora pointed out.

"That's true . . ." Stella said.

"And think about how fun it will be!" Cora smiled, bouncing in place on her bed.

"Yes but—"

"Yes but *what*?" Cora leapt to her feet on the bed, tossing the blanket aside as she really started to bounce. "What could be more adventurous than sneaking down to Wishworld? With your best friend! It would be the greatest pre-graduation bonding moment known to Starling Academy—and really, all of Starland itself! It's something we'll be able to talk about for the rest of our lives! To tell our children! Or maybe something *not* to tell our children—the most treasured secret that only the two of us know! Plus, you'll get the chance to test out those Wishworld Relations theories even if you don't use the findings in your project! Come on, say yes!"

Stella laughed as Cora pulled her up and got her to start bouncing, too. "You're crazy! We can't possibly do it!"

"We can't possibly *not!*" Cora insisted—and the higher they bounced, the clearer it became to both of them.

"Okay . . . let's go!" Stella finally agreed, collapsing onto the bed. "But we'd better not get caught."

"We won't," Cora assured her best friend as they lay there side by side, completely out of breath.

Now all they needed to do was figure out how to get down to Wishworld and back to Starland again without anybody finding out. But Cora was certain that between the two of them, they could make it happen.

The dark sky was glowing with countless tiny stars as Stella and Cora stood on the rooftop deck of the Big Dipper Dormitory. All the other students at Starling Academy had long since gone to bed, making it the perfect time for the girls to catch a shooting star without being seen. Star Wrangling had always been one of Stella's favorite elective classes. At first, it had seemed almost impossible to gather enough wish energy to get the dynamic and unpredictable practice stars under control, but in a short time she'd mastered the skill. That said, as much as the idea of sneaking down to Wishworld with her best friend excited Stella, she was still sorting out some of the other logistics.

"I seriously can't believe we're doing this!" Stella widened her eyes, crossing and hugging her arms against her chest as she shivered, both from the cool night air and the nervous energy she'd been feeling ever since Cora had proposed the expedition.

"I know," Cora replied with a shrewd smile as she slowly walked toward the edge of the deck, her head tilted back so she could search the sky for shooting stars. "But if you weren't a bit worried, it wouldn't be worth it! It wouldn't be as exciting! It wouldn't be an adventure!"

Stella shook her head and laughed in spite of herself. Cora had a way of making everything sound perfectly logical and entirely appealing—even something no Starling without a wish-granting degree was ever supposed to attempt.

"But how do we know that these pendants are going to work on the real Wishworld?" Stella asked, lightly touching the glowing pink sphere that hung from a delicate gold chain around her neck. It was the one she used in Practice Wish Orb Mastery class, and Cora was wearing the sparkly gold star ring that she used in her class.

"We don't," Cora said, glancing at Stella with a shrug, as if the pendants weren't an essential part of every journey to Wishworld. "But we decided we're not going down there to try to find a specific Wisher or test out any theories—we're just going to check the place out."

"True." Stella nodded.

"Although"—Cora added mischievously—"if all goes well, would it be so bad to encourage a couple of girls who've lost hope to wish for something really big? Like I said before, we don't *have* to test out the theories, but you never know what might happen. That's part of what makes this so incredible: we're venturing into the great unknown!"

Stella felt a warm glow rise to her cheeks at the mention of testing out their Wishworld Relations ideas—and then, once again, an inkling of doubt crept in. "But we need to be able to disguise ourselves," she pointed out. "If we can't use our pendants as cloaking devices, we won't be able to blend in with the Wishlings."

"Then I guess we'll just have to hope for the best," Cora insisted, her blue eyes sparkling in the starlight.

Stella sighed and forced herself to smile. Cora was right: a little bit of worrying was fine, but she needed to focus on all the positives of what they were about to do. It *was* pretty exciting—not only because she was going on a super-secret adventure with her best friend, and not just because she was finally going to see what the *real* Wishworld was like, but because she and Cora would finally, hopefully, get to see each other disguised as Wishlings and maybe, just maybe, get some sense of whether she was on the right track with her Wish-Science Fair project.

"You're right," Stella said, skipping over to Cora and gazing up into the dark sky. Almost as soon as she reached the edge of the deck, a shimmering stream of light zipped overhead. It was a shooting star, and it was headed directly for the girls.

"It's time!" Cora squealed, and reached out to grab Stella's hand as she slid on the blue-framed star safety glasses she used during Star Wrangling class. "Are you ready to make the lasso?"

"Yes—I think so." Stella shivered again as she quickly put on her own pink star safety glasses and began to focus every bit of her attention on sweeping up a sparkling cloud of wish energy from the surface of the rooftop deck. It took all the strength she and Cora could muster to swirl the energy into a giant silver lasso.

"That's it," Cora whispered excitedly. "Now throw it!"

Stella swiftly dropped her head back and narrowed her eyes behind her safety glasses, using as much energy manipulation as possible to toss the lasso. As she did so, it encircled and tightened around the shooting star just as it whooshed above her. "Oh, my stars, Cora!" Stella screamed, nearly thrown off balance by the powerful star. "This one is really powerful! I'm not sure I can hang on to it!"

"Don't worry," Cora replied—and as Stella kept her eyes trained on the lasso, she almost immediately noticed that it became steady thanks to Cora's assisting with her own energy manipulation skills. Finally, the lasso stopped shaking and both girls slowly but surely pulled the shooting star down toward the deck.

"Got it?" Stella asked, still completely focused on the glowing yellow star.

"Just about," Cora replied through gritted teeth. "Okay, let's get on!"

Stella sucked in her breath as she and Cora both reached out and grabbed hold of the star. Once they were in place and securely attached with the lasso of wish energy, the star took off at lightning speed.

"Whoa!" they screamed as they went flying through the sky and down, down, down toward Wishworld.

"It's just like the Star Mountain ride at Glitzyland!" Cora shouted.

"Only way better!" Stella yelled back, closing her eyes happily as the wind whipped through her long golden-pink hair and she thought about the first time she and Cora had gone to the famous glowmusement park together to celebrate Cora's Bright Day with her family. They had been too scared to go on Star Mountain or the Glitterhorn—the two fastest star coaster rides there— but ultimately, Cora's brother Cosmo convinced them that they would regret it if they didn't at least try. And he had been right: as soon as they exited that first ride, they couldn't wait to go again . . . and again. Sometimes, when coming up against challenges in the time since, Stella would think about that day and how exhilarating it felt to face and conquer her fears—and now she and Cora were doing it again. They were going on the scariest but most exciting ride of their lives!

Before Stella knew it, she and Cora were approaching Wishworld—and as the ground came into view, she felt her Star-Zap buzzing. She pulled up the antenna and saw the words COMMENCE APPEARANCE CHANGE, exactly like it happened in Practice Wish Orb Mastery class.

"Cora! Are you getting an appearance change message on your Star-Zap?" Stella asked.

"Yes!" Cora replied. "It must be programmed to do that any time it gets close to Wishworld's atmosphere."

"Of course," Stella mused, slightly disappointed in herself for not realizing that was what might happen.

Then she saw that the Wishworld Outfit Selector on her Star-Zap was also working like it did in Practice Wish Orb Mastery class, and she quickly changed from her sparkly pink dress, leggings, and boots into a plain pink dress with a white collar and a pair of simple white sneakers. She looked at Cora and saw that she, too, had changed, from her bright blue dress into a pleated skirt in pale blue with a matching short-sleeved sweater and shoes.

"Okay, let's give this a try," Cora called to Stella as they both clutched their Wish Pendants tightly and closed their eyes.

Then, in unison, they both said, "Star light, star bright, the first star I see tonight: I wish I may, I wish I might, have the wish I wish tonight."

As Stella imagined her shiny golden-pink ponytail changing to light brown, she looked down at her hands and arms and saw that all the glitter and sparkle was disappearing from her skin, just as she had pictured.

"It's working, Cora!" she squealed, looking at her best friend, whose long light blue hair was now pale yellow. Cora's skin had also become smooth and dull.

"Wow—you look different," Cora said to Stella as their star touched down at the edge of a huge field with rows upon rows of green plants that were almost as tall as the girls.

"So do you!" Stella couldn't stop staring at Cora. "You look just like a Wishling."

"Thanks. I think?" Cora smiled as she took off her safety glasses, revealing pale blue eyes that were *almost* like her real ones, only far less shiny.

Stella took off her glasses, too, and both girls watched as their shooting star sputtered out and became still on the ground. Cora bent down to pick it up, then carefully folded it and put it in a little white purse that hung from a strap on her shoulder.

"You'd better not lose that," Stella said as a pang of fear made her stomach drop. "We wouldn't want to be stuck here."

"Don't worry, it's safe," Cora insisted with a confident smile. "Come on—let's check this place out and see if we can find a Wisher!"

Stella nodded, reassured, and glanced around at the spot where they had landed. Her eyes widened as she and Cora began to walk along a dirt trail past the outer row of plants, which seemed to go on as far as the eye could see. She flinched a bit as she touched the long slightly rough and prickly leaves that shot out from each thick stalk.

"I can't believe these are *real* Wishworld plants and not practice ones!" Stella marveled.

"And look how many there are," Cora said, looking all around as she continued to lead the way along the path.

"Where should we go?" Stella asked.

"I'm not sure," Cora replied. "But that building over there looks interesting. Maybe it's a Wishworld house."

She pointed to a bright red structure with a white roof that curved over the top of it, almost like a bonnet.

Beneath the roof were two square white windows and a wide opening at the bottom where it seemed like a door should be. Running alongside the building was a stretch of black pavement leading out to a road—and beyond that was a small white path winding up to a gray house with a black roof. The house and the red structure seemed to be the only two buildings around. Beyond that was nothing but rolling hills covered in soft-looking green and yellow grass. As she continued to follow Cora, Stella looked up at the sky, which was almost the same blue as her best friend's eyes and full of fluffy white clouds. She couldn't believe she and Cora had been flying above those very clouds moments earlier.

"Ew, what is that *smell*?" Cora asked in a loud whisper when they finally arrived at the opening to the red building. She pinched her nose with her fingers and grimaced as she turned to look at Stella.

"Ugh—stinkberries?" Stella whispered back, also pinching her nose. "I think it's coming from inside this building."

"Well, then I hope this isn't a Wishling house," Cora said. "Because I would hate to discover that real Wishlings smell like stinkberries."

Stella giggled. She was certain it couldn't be a Wishling smell. Surely Starland scientists would have made the ones in the practice Wish Orbs smell the same way if that was the case . . . wouldn't they?

"It must be something else," Stella said, creeping ahead of Cora and taking a few tentative steps inside. As she did, thick pieces of yellow grass crunched loudly under her sneakers—loudly enough that they apparently disturbed whatever was living inside.

"Oh, my stars—what was that?" Cora gasped at the strange sound, leaping up right behind Stella and grabbing her hand.

"I don't know," Stella whispered, her stomach in knots. "It sounded kind of like a galliope!"

As nervous as she was, and as disgusting as it smelled in there, Stella couldn't resist the urge to keep exploring. She clutched Cora's hand like a security blanket and dragged her along until, yes, sure enough, they were standing outside a wooden fence with what appeared to be a galliope inside! It was large, with a long tail and a mane. The only difference was that this creature was dark brown instead of the more colorful and shimmering hues that galliopes on Starland were—and instead of being shy and standoffish, it seemed happy to see them.

"Whoa," Stella and Cora both sighed as they looked into its big dark eyes and watched it try to poke its nose through the slats of wood in the gate.

Stella reached out to pat its head. "Look, Cora," she

said, noticing the white star-shaped marking between its ears.

"A star," Cora said, her voice full of awe. "I wonder if that's some sort of sign."

"I don't know, but I just remembered something from back in our Wishers 101 class," Stella said.

"What?"

"This isn't a galliope—on Wishworld, it's called a horse!"

"Ah!" Cora nodded. "You're right. I can't believe you remembered that."

"You know what else?" Stella grinned and pointed at the horse as it backed off into a corner and began releasing a horrible pile of big round pellets onto the ground. "Apparently they make giant stinkberries!"

At that, the girls both burst into fits of laughter.

"Oh, Cora, this was such a good idea—coming to Wishworld," Stella said between giggles. "Even if we don't meet a single Wishling, being down here with you is more than enough for me."

"Me too," Cora said, her eyes becoming shiny with happy tears. "But I *do* want to see if we can find a few Wishlings—and I also really want to get away from the smell of stinkberries. Sorry, galliope—er, I mean horse!"

Stella giggled and agreed. "But," she said as they walked back to the big open doorway, "it seems like this place is really isolated, like not many Wishlings live around here."

"Do you think we should knock on the door to the house?" Cora asked when they got outside.

"Sure, let's give it a try," Stella replied. But before they even had a chance to head toward it, she saw the door to the house open—and a girl about the same age as them slammed it, then ran down the front steps and raced in their direction.

"Quick! Get back inside!" Stella whispered to Cora, pulling her back into the red building while scanning the place for a good spot to hide. She did want to meet the Wishling girl—*maybe*—but first they needed to come up with a way to introduce themselves.

As she looked around, she noticed that the yellow grass scattered all over the ground had also been gathered into what looked like giant cubes—and a whole bunch of them were stacked on top of each other in a far corner. "Come on, let's go over there!" Stella said. Once they were safely behind the yellow cubes, she widened her eyes at Cora and whispered, "What do you think we should do? What sort of explanation can we give her about why we're here?"

Cora frowned and shook her head, deep in thought. "Oh!" she finally whispered back. "Maybe we can tell her we're visiting from out of town and we went on a walk and got lost?"

"Yes—that could work." Stella breathed a little sigh of relief. It sounded like a perfectly logical explanation, and if anyone could make it convincing, it was Cora. Her acting skills would be a seriously useful asset on Wishworld.

But just as she and Cora were about to step out and introduce themselves, they heard not only footsteps crunching quickly on the ground inside, but the sound of the girl crying so hard that her sobs sounded like *cry-gasp-hiccup, cry-gasp-hiccup*. Stella pulled Cora back to their hiding spot and grabbed her hand urgently. "Should we really go out there? She sounds so upset."

"Yes," Cora whispered back. "That's exactly why we *should* go out there—maybe we can help her."

So they crept out from their hiding place and tiptoed toward the horse's stall, where the girl was now standing.

"Oh, Chestnut, what are we going to do?" the girl sobbed—to the horse, apparently—not noticing that Stella and Cora were just a few steps away.

Her thick black hair was braided and tied up neatly in the back, and even though her face had become red and blotchy from crying, she was still lovely, with dark eyes and thick lashes. She wore a pair of light brown pants tucked into black boots, which came up to her knees, and a crisp white button-down shirt. She opened the gate to get inside the stall with the horse and threw her arms around its neck as she continued to cry. "We're never going to stop them from letting Jimmy ride you in that race! *What will I do?*"

Stella shot a questioning glance over her shoulder at Cora. Should they interrupt the girl's moment with her horse? Stella felt bad for listening in on something that seemed so private and sad. Before Stella could decide what to do, Cora cleared her throat loudly—and that got the girl's attention.

"Who's there?" the girl asked, panic in her voice.

Cora stepped to the stall gate, taking Stella by the hand and pulling her along. "Hi—sorry to creep up on you," Cora replied gently. "I'm Cora, and this is my friend Stella."

"Oh!" The girl quickly used the back of her hand to wipe away her tears. "Where did you come from? I mean—why are you here?"

"We're visiting some friends from up the road and got a bit lost when we decided to go for a walk," Stella said, sticking to the story Cora had proposed.

"What friends?" the girl asked, narrowing her eyes as if she didn't believe them.

"It's . . . um . . . the Brown family," Stella quickly replied, inspired by the color of the horse.

The girl nodded as she considered that. "Are they the family that just moved into the Millers' old place—up on Williams Road?"

"Yes!" Stella and Cora both said at once.

"Well, that was a long walk, then. You're *really* lost!" The girl seemed more impressed than suspicious.

"It was," Cora agreed with a smile.

"Can you give us directions back there?" Stella asked.

"Sure," the girl agreed, patting the horse's long neck before coming out of the stall and closing the latch behind her.

"Oh—but wait," Cora said, discreetly tapping Stella's hand. "We don't have to go just yet. We *love* horses. Did you say his name is Chestnut?"

"Yeah." The girl looked back into the stall and tears began to well in her eyes again. "That's Chestnut—and I'm Amy."

"It's nice to meet you, Amy." Stella smiled.

"Yes, nice to meet you," Cora added. "Um . . . I know we just met, but can I ask why you were crying? I heard you say something about someone named Jimmy."

"Cora!" Stella gave her friend a stern look. She knew exactly what Cora was doing: trying to figure out if there might be a way for them to test out their Wishworld Relations theory and somehow encourage Amy to make a good wish. But they had just met her, and Stella wasn't sure they should pry about something that was clearly upsetting her.

"Oh—it's okay." Amy smiled weakly at Stella and blinked back her tears. "I don't mind talking about it, especially if you love horses. . . ."

"We do! Love them!" Cora insisted.

"Have you ever competed in a race?" Amy asked.

"No." Cora shook her head and gave Stella's hand another secret pat. "Where we come from, girls aren't allowed to race competitively."

Of course Cora wasn't telling the truth; girls on Starland were considered to be some of the best galliope racers around. In fact, Stella's friend Celeste had a wall covered in ribbons from all of her races. Plus, a lot of young Starling girls were obsessed with galliopes and some kept them as pets.

"That's exactly why I'm so sad," Amy revealed. "I've been working so hard to get Chestnut ready for the summer meet next month, and now my parents have hired a cruel, horrible jockey named Jimmy to ride him instead of me."

"Oh, no." Stella frowned. She knew that Celeste would *never* want someone else to compete on one of her galliopes—especially someone cruel and horrible.

"There must be some way you can change their

minds," Cora said. "Do they know how terrible this Jimmy person is—or that you're the one who's been getting Chestnut ready, that you want to ride him?"

"They know all about Jimmy *and* they know I want to ride Chestnut, but they won't let me," Amy replied with a sigh. "I don't know how to convince them. I don't think I can."

"There must be a way," Stella said.

"There isn't," Amy said softly, staring at the ground. "They've always said that female jockeys aren't strong enough competitors."

Stella grabbed Cora's hand and squeezed it. As sad as she was for Amy, she was also incredibly excited about how her situation perfectly mirrored everything they'd discussed in Wishworld Relations about girls being told they're not as capable as boys. Just like the star ball player in Stella's example, Amy had given up hope. This was Stella's opportunity to prove her theory—if she could just help Amy believe in herself enough for her to make a good wish!

"But *you* know you're a strong enough competitor ... right?" Stella asked.

"I'm honestly not even sure anymore," Amy replied. "If my own parents don't have faith in me, why should I?"

"Because this is your heart's desire," Stella said.

"And maybe you're an even better rider than Jimmy."

"Exactly!" Cora added. "You're probably *a lot* better than Jimmy. You just need to be given a chance."

"Yes," Amy sighed, tears flowing from her dark eyes again. "You're right. He's not as good as I am, and truly, Chestnut can't stand him. *I* can't stand him."

"Why not?" Cora asked, giving Stella's hand yet another enthusiastic tap.

"Oh, you might not even believe me if I told you," Amy said, the small amount of color in her face draining away.

"Of course we'll believe you," Cora insisted.

Amy shook her head and sighed again, but then she slowly began to list all the terrible things Jimmy had done to poor Chestnut and some of the other horses he had ridden in the past—forcing them to sleep in dirty stalls and depriving them of food after losing races. It was all so awful it made Stella feel even queasier than the smell of stinkberries did.

"He was even banned from racing for a while because he used his whip so much that his horse needed to be given oxygen after one of his meets!" Amy revealed.

"Oh, my goodness," Cora gasped. "That's awful. You *have* to do something to stop him from riding Chestnut!"

"You're right." Amy nodded. "I know you're right."

"So let's think of a way," Cora said. "How can you stop him?"

"I'm not sure." Amy scowled and shook her head. "I feel like something really bad would have to happen."

"Or something good," Stella replied, suddenly realizing that the conversation had taken a far different turn than she had anticipated.

"Well, yes, but for something *good* to happen—like me riding Chestnut—something *bad* would have to happen to Jimmy," Amy insisted.

"Like what?" Cora asked eagerly.

"Honestly, sometimes I wish Chestnut would just trample him!" Amy blurted out.

No!

The moment Amy said that, Stella felt like she'd been punched in the stomach—like all the air had been sucked out of the room and the ground had fallen from beneath her feet. But then it got even worse: a dark gray cloud of negative wish energy—visible only to Stella and Cora—swirled all around Amy, circling her several times before turning into a horrible, toxic ball. Stella was certain she heard it scream as it made its final transformation into a Bad Wish Orb and shot out of the building.

Stella grabbed Cora's hand and they looked at each other, wide-eyed, in terror, both trembling uncontrollably.

Stella felt like she might actually faint. After all, she knew that the Bad Wish Orb was on its way to Starland and it was all because of the secret journey she had taken with Cora. Of course, Wishlings made bad wishes every once and a while, but that she was responsible for one was unthinkable for Stella. Plus, if anyone found out, it could ruin her chances of joining the prestigious Wish-Tank.

Once they made their way onto Starland, Bad Wish Orbs were contained in the Negative Energy Facility, or NEF for short, in hopes they would never come true. But Stella knew that if this one did somehow come true on its own, it would be at least partly her fault.

If they hadn't gone down to Wishworld, perhaps Amy never would have made that bad wish. But now she had and there was no turning back. Stella knew that she and Cora needed to get out of there—to return to Starland—as soon as possible and find a way to undo the damage. But how?

8

Cora couldn't bear to look at Stella once they had landed safely back on the rooftop of the Big Dipper Dormitory. She wasn't sure if it was some sort of residual effect of having transformed into a Wishling or the extreme speed at which they had traveled through the atmosphere, but she felt like all the sparkle had been drained from her system. Deep down, as much as she was afraid to even think it, she also wondered if she had been stripped of her glow because of what had happened with Amy—because of the bad wish the girl had made. The bad wish that Cora couldn't help feeling was almost entirely her fault.

The terrifying images were still fresh in Cora's mind: as she and Stella had stood there with Amy, and Cora had encouraged her to come up with a way to stop the jockey from riding her horse, Amy suddenly uttered those fateful words—"I wish Chestnut would just trample him!"—and the negative energy almost immediately consumed her. Cora and Stella had been determined to inspire Amy to make a *good* wish, but the moment the Bad Wish Orb had formed, they both knew it was too late.

Cora had done all she could—told Amy to take back the wish, tried to explain to her that if any harm ever did come to the jockey, it couldn't possibly make her feel better and might even make her feel worse. Stella had also tried to steer Amy back to making a good wish. But there was an intense fire burning in Amy's dark eyes at that point. There was no way she would shift her focus back to believing in herself, wishing for something positive to happen. She was too intent on seeing the jockey fail, not to mention punishing her parents for not believing in her. "I'll make them see that they picked the wrong person to ride Chestnut!" Amy had sworn. "I'll make them regret this!"

Fearing that things would only get worse, Cora and Stella had no choice but to leave Wishworld. As they waved good-bye to Amy, they did their best to channel as much positive energy as possible to her—hoping against hope that it might help change her bad wish into a good one. Then, after Amy pointed them in the direction of the house they had said they were visiting, Cora and Stella walked along the dusty road until they were safely out of sight. Cora unfolded the star that had taken them on their disastrous Wishworld journey, and—without speaking a word to each other—she and Stella returned to Starland.

"What are we going to do?" Stella asked, her voice barely above a whisper, as they stood on the rooftop deck. "Our energy will be all over that Bad Wish Orb."

Cora shook her head and sucked in her breath, her chest feeling tight and heavy from stress. The whole thing was her fault. If she hadn't proposed that she and Stella sneak down to Wishworld, and if she hadn't pressed Amy to come up with a way to stop the horrible jockey from riding that horse, none of it would have happened. Cora knew what she had to do, but she was afraid to say it. Finally, she looked into her best friend's frightened eyes and spoke up.

"I'm going to go to the Negative Energy Facility," Cora said. "I'm going to find that Bad Wish Orb and I'm going to find a way to destroy it!"

"Oh, Cora, no!" Stella shook her head and looked even more terrified. "You can't possibly! It's too dangerous! You'll never be able to get in there, anyway. How would you?"

"I don't know, but I have to try," Cora insisted. "I'm the one to blame for it."

"Cora..." Stella reached out and grabbed her friend's hand. "It was as much my fault as yours. I agreed that we should sneak down to Wishworld. I was right there with you, trying to help guide Amy toward making a good wish."

"Yes, but *I* convinced you to take the trip and *I* was the one who encouraged Amy to come up with a way to stop the horrible jockey. If I hadn't agreed with her when she was being so negative, maybe she wouldn't have made that...that *bad wish*!" Cora dropped Stella's hand and walked to the edge of the rooftop deck. She stared up at the dark sky and wondered what would happen to her, and to Stella, if she didn't find and somehow destroy that Bad Wish Orb.

A few moments later, Stella walked up behind her and placed a hand softly on her shoulder. "What's done is done, Cora—we can't take it back," she insisted. "Going to the Negative Energy Facility isn't an option. There's no way I can let you do that."

Cora spun around to face her friend and knew it was going to be impossible to convince her—even though Cora remained certain that going to the Negative Energy Facility was their only option.

Cora finally relented. "Okay. But I'm going to come up with a plan. I have to."

"No, *we'll* come up with a plan," Stella replied firmly. "But not now. We need to try to get some sleep. We can figure all of this out in the morning—well, later this morning."

Cora sighed and nodded reluctantly. But as she and Stella made their way through the door leading back into the Big Dipper Dormitory, and headed down the glass staircase to their room, she knew there was no way she would be able to get any sleep.

After they had used their toothlights and changed into their pajamas, Cora gave Stella a quick hug and watched her head up the staircase to bed. Of course Cora wanted to fall asleep—to let good dreams replace all the lingering memories of the trouble she had caused—but as she lay beneath her covers, she was more awake than ever. Feelings of guilt and regret were squeezing her heart so hard that she could barely breathe. She had to do something. It simply couldn't wait.

So Cora pushed back her soft blue blanket, got out of bed, and quickly changed into her favorite navy-blue leggings, boots, and a long sweater. Then she pulled on a blue knit cap and tiptoed to the staircase leading up to Stella's bed, where she waited until she could hear the sounds of her friend's deep, rhythmic breathing—the unmistakable sign that she was fast asleep. Once Cora was certain that Stella wouldn't catch her, she headed out.

The journey to the Negative Energy Facility was a long one, but Cora hoped she could make it there and back before Stella woke up. The prospect of being able to give her friend good news later that morning kept her going, providing her the energy she needed to travel at the swiftest pace possible. As she walked along the quiet roads, bathed in shimmering moonlight, she followed the route on her Star-Zap and soon found herself heading through Dimtown, located on the outskirts of Starland City. Unlike on the rest of Starland, the homes and buildings and even the plants, trees, and Starlings who lived in the region were slightly muted, lacking the vibrant colors and sparkle found elsewhere. It was the first sign that she was getting closer to her destination.

Finally, Cora came to a small hill covered in dry brown grass, and when she reached the top, she could see a dark, ominous cave in the distance. Her heart felt heavy with dread as she checked the Star-Zap to confirm what she suspected: inside that cave was the Negative Energy Facility. It was the most desolate and terrifying place on all of Starland—the sort of place that Starlings spoke about only rarely, in hushed tones or while trying to scare each other as they gathered around a campfire, telling ghost stories.

The area wasn't slightly shadowy like Dimtown, nor did it glow like the rest of Starland. Instead, the jagged cliffs surrounding the cave smoldered in hues of sinister blue and gray, and the plants growing out of the dusty ground were shriveled and gnarled, as if negative energy had somehow seeped out of the facility and consumed them all. Cora shuddered as she realized that perhaps it had—that maybe the air was indeed heavy and thick with a toxic force and if she got any closer, it might swallow her up, too!

As apprehensive as she was, Cora slowly made her way down the hill and followed the long, winding path leading toward the cave. She caught her breath when she finally arrived at the cave's craggy opening. Peering inside, she could see the entirety of the Negative Energy Facility towering above her. Rising from its perilously sharp rocky base was an enormous tear-shaped dome that swirled in shades of purple and indigo, with dark, bruised, disease-like spots. Its vaulted form was a physical manifestation of its misery, as it seemed to lurch and wail from the pain of all the Bad Wish Orbs it contained.

Trembling, Cora wondered if she could really accomplish what she had set out to do. What if Stella was right—what if she wasn't able to get inside the facility? At least when they went down to Wishworld, they had learned enough about the place in their classes to be somewhat prepared for what they would find and how they could navigate it. But this was *truly* the great unknown—the NEF was a place that no books or classes had ever prepared her for. All she knew was that it was to be avoided at all costs.

As Cora crept closer to the facility, she saw that the heavy black iron door had an enormous combination security lock. She got closer and began punching in numbers, but it was no use. How was she going to crack the code? There was no way. Already glimpsing her defeat, she decided she shouldn't have made the journey after all—but as she neared the opening of the cave, she saw a vehicle kicking up a cloud of dust, and it was heading straight toward her! Who could it be and why would they be heading for the Negative Energy Facility? Moreover, what would they do if they saw Cora there? With her pulse racing, she quickly ducked behind a large rock. It was her only option, as the vehicle was getting closer and she wouldn't be able to slip by without being caught in its headlights.

Cora sucked in her breath as the vehicle slowly drove past her hiding spot. It was an enormous yellow truck with painted black letters spelling out "B.W.O.T. ~ BAD

WISH ORB TRANSPORT" on the side. It drove right up to the door of the Negative Energy Facility, and two male Starlings, along with an enormous Armored Law Enforcement Bot-Bot, emerged. The Starlings wore glowing yellow hooded jumpsuits and heavy black boots, and Cora assumed they were Bad Wish Orb Gatherers. Meanwhile, the armored Bot-Bot was taller than any Cora had ever seen before, with big silver plates covering its mechanical arms and legs, huge black wheels for feet, and glowing purple eyes.

All three headed to the back of the truck, where one of the Wish Gatherers flung open the doors to reveal a crate with several Bad Wish Orbs—each one crackling and glowing in sinister purple hues and, worse, making awful wailing noises. That was when Cora was almost certain she heard the unmistakable sobs—the same *cry-gasp-hiccup*—that she and Stella had heard when they first met Amy down on Wishworld! Could they actually *be* Amy's cries, coming from inside her Bad Wish Orb? Cora knew she had to find out—but how? The Armored Law Enforcement Bot-Bot was quite literally attached to the crate of Bad Wish Orbs so it could transport them inside. There was no way Cora could get near them while he was there.

Squeezing her eyes shut, Cora searched her heart

and mind for a strategy—something, *anything*, that would allow her to get to that Bad Wish Orb. Then it came to her: she would need to get close enough to observe the Wish Gatherers as they entered the code to open the door to the Negative Energy Facility, so she could gain access after they left and *then* find Amy's Bad Wish Orb! So she began to focus all her energy on levitating, just as she and Stella had practiced many times before. Slowly but surely, she rose off the ground and stealthily floated to the facility entrance, where the Wish Gatherers were about to punch in the code that would open the door. The moment they began pressing the buttons on the silver keypad, Cora memorized the sequence. That was it! Now all she had to do was wait until they finished putting the Bad Wish Orbs inside and left—and then she would finally get her chance to undo all the damage she'd done on that fateful journey to Wishworld.

With the code committed to memory, Cora returned to her hiding place and waited for the Wish Gatherers and the armored Bot-Bot to complete their work. At last, they emerged from the Negative Energy Facility, slid the door closed and locked it behind them, and then climbed into their vehicle. After they'd driven a safe distance away, Cora steeled herself for what she was about to do. It was time.

Although her hands were shaking almost uncontrollably when she got to the door, Cora managed to enter the lock code as the Wish Gatherers had, and breathed a sigh of relief when she heard the clicking sound of the heavy bolt releasing. Her pale blue eyes widened as she carefully slid the door open a crack and peered inside, where a fine mist of gray fog swirled all around and the awful sounds of moaning and wailing were louder than ever. Realizing how heavy the door was, she suddenly worried that it might slide closed behind her—and she might be trapped inside the Negative Energy Facility forever! She had to do something to make sure that wouldn't happen. Scanning the ground, which was littered with shiny bits of black rock and debris, she zeroed in on a piece of rock large enough to hold the door open. It was only about the size of her hand, but it would do the trick. When she reached down to grab it, she noticed it was uncomfortably icy to the touch but also quite solid. So she quickly used it to wedge the door open a crack, confident that it would remain that way until she was ready to leave the facility.

Then, as frightened as she was, Cora headed inside, careful not to disturb the orbs. The farther she went, the more a force seemed to be pulling at her—and she was more certain than ever that she could hear Amy's distinctive sobs. So she slowly made her way past one

Bad Wish Orb after another, each glassy black sphere crackling and glowing with terrifying purple sparks as it ducked and bobbed, struggling to stay afloat in the noxious air.

At last Cora arrived at the spot where the sound of Amy's cries seemed to be the loudest, and one of the orbs began circling her head, hissing and glowing with a tortured purple aura as its sobs grew louder and then louder still. That was the one! It had to be Amy's Bad Wish Orb! It must have recognized Cora and pulled her toward it somehow—and as alarming as that realization was, it also made her task clearer: she had to destroy it.

Cora thought about everything she'd learned in Practice Wish Orb Mastery class. Could she get inside this orb the same way she did with the practice ones? But if she did that, would she be able to destroy the bad wish—or would she simply return to the spot where she and Stella had met Amy, where they had already failed to reverse, let alone destroy, the bad wish? Although the answers remained unclear, Cora suddenly felt compelled to take hold of the orb.

As Cora's hands came into contact with its surface, she felt prickly jolts like it was shocking her, and the sounds of Amy's cries grew even louder until they became a scream so deafening that Cora thought she might not be able to hold on any longer. She wrapped her fingers around the orb, clutching it as tightly as possible. But that only caused it to quake and shock her with an even greater force until, suddenly, it exploded! Cora watched in horror as glassy shards flew in every direction and a massive terrifying cloud of gray fog was released. Then Cora was the one screaming and crying as the poisonous mist began to circle her like a tornado—just as it had Amy on Wishworld. After what felt like an eternity, the fog finally left her and proceeded to writhe and slither toward the open doorway of the Negative Energy Facility like a huge, hideous serpent.

Until that moment, Cora had been frozen in place, paralyzed with fear. But as she watched the cloud of negative energy heading for the outside world, the fear she felt was gone. She watched with a detached interest as the toxic cloud escaped, sliding through the crack in the doorway into the Starland atmosphere.

Cora felt a chill run down her spine, like a jolt of dark electricity. She walked toward the door, then quickly bent down to grab the black rock that had been keeping it wedged open. Without even thinking about why, she placed it in the pocket of her sweater. As she did so, she felt a surprising surge of power.

Next Cora slid through the doorway and headed out

of the facility, stopping only long enough to close the door and secure the lock before making her way out of the cave. It wasn't until she got to the outside path that she discovered she wasn't alone. There, standing by the boulder where Cora had hidden from the Bad Wish Orb transport vehicle, was Stella!

9

As she watched Cora walking away from the Negative Energy Facility, Stella felt like her legs might buckle beneath her. She didn't know what was more frightening—the fact that she'd found her best friend in one of the most treacherous places on all of Starland, or that a huge cloud of negative energy had blown out of the facility and almost directly into Stella as soon as she arrived.

"Stella!" Cora gasped, and flung her arms around her friend. "What are you doing here?"

Stella pulled away from Cora and tried to reconcile the conflicting emotions she was feeling—fury over her best friend's doing something so reckless, relief that she had made it out of the facility without any obvious damage, and worry that she might have been harmed in some way. Concern finally won out as Stella grabbed Cora's hands.

"I wanted to make sure you were okay," she said. "Are you?"

"I think so!" Cora nodded with a fiery look in her pale blue eyes as she slowly pulled the knit cap off her head, revealing a tangled mess of long, shimmering blue hair. "I think I found Amy's orb, Stella—and I got rid of it!"

"Really? That's great," Stella said with a weak smile. It was hard for her to focus on Cora's victory without also acknowledging what had gone wrong. "I thought we agreed that you weren't going to come here, though."

"I know," Cora replied. "But I couldn't sleep—and the more I thought about it, the more I realized this was our only option."

Stella shook her head, fighting back the tears of frustration and rage that were beginning to burn her eyes. "You should have waited for me!"

"I couldn't—I knew you wouldn't agree to come." Cora frowned with a bitter intensity unlike anything Stella had ever seen before.

"You're right," Stella acknowledged, turning away from her friend and shivering as she looked at the jagged cliffs of the cave. "But when I saw that you were headed in this direction, I didn't exactly have a choice."

"How did you know I was coming here?" Cora asked. "You were asleep when I left."

"Yes, I was." Stella nodded, gently closing her eyes and wishing that she'd never left the safety and comfort of her bed and dorm room—and that Cora hadn't, either. Finally, she turned back around to face her friend. "But I had a nightmare. About Amy. It was so terrible that it woke me up, and when I went downstairs to tell you about it, you were gone. I was so worried! When I searched for you on my Friend Finder and saw where you were going, I came as fast as I could."

"Well, we don't need to worry about Amy anymore." Cora tossed her head triumphantly. "That nightmare is over and done with for good."

"But, Cora," Stella said, widening her eyes at her friend. "Didn't you see what happened? Didn't you see that gust of gray fog escaping from the facility?"

Stella felt her stomach lurch as she thought about how close the thick, horrible cloud had come to her. It was far more awful than the Bad Wish Orb that had nearly hit her on the way to the Celestial Café the previous day.

"Oh, that," Cora said with a shrug. "Yes, I saw it."

"Don't you realize what it was?" Stella asked.

"I guess it was a bit of negative energy," Cora replied, glancing back at the facility.

"A *bit*?" Stella barked, growing more furious by the moment. "It was huge! And now it's out in the Starland atmosphere!" Then concern for her friend won out again. "It didn't touch you, did it?"

"I . . . don't think so." Cora shook her head, but Stella suddenly noticed that her face had lost some of its shine, and even her hair and clothes had less sparkle to them.

"Are you *sure*?" Stella asked, examining her friend more closely. "Because there's something different about you."

"There is?" Cora blinked her eyes innocently and stood a bit taller.

"I don't know—maybe not." Stella ran a hand over Cora's hair, trying to smooth it out, and breathed a sigh of relief as it started to shimmer again.

"I'm telling you, Stella, everything's fine," Cora insisted. "I got here right when the Wish Gatherers were bringing in a new crate of Bad Wish Orbs—and I heard one that I'm certain was crying in the exact way Amy did when we met her on Wishworld! So I grabbed it and broke it. It's gone!"

"Hmmm." Stella had to admit she was impressed that Cora had been so brave—and that she'd managed to do what Stella had truly believed would be impossible. But she still couldn't shake the terrifying image of that cloud of negative energy escaping from the facility. "Well, I guess I should be grateful to you for all that—but destroying a Bad Wish Orb created a negative energy leak. And you know we have to report the leak now . . . right?"

"No!" Cora shook her head forcefully. "That would be a huge mistake!"

Stella sucked in her breath, cringing at the thought of what all those toxins might do—might already be doing—to Starland. "Cora, we don't have a choice."

"Yes, we do," Cora insisted. "It's one small leak. We can keep it a secret—just like our trip to Wishworld!"

Stella took one of Cora's hands in hers. "I know you're scared," she said softly. "I'm scared, too. But we can't possibly keep something like this a secret."

"I'm not scared!" Cora fired back. "I took care of the problem—and if we tell anyone about the negative energy escaping, we'll only be creating a new one. They'll want to know what we were doing here in the first place, and if they press us hard enough, we might even have to confess to sneaking down to Wishworld. *Both* of us sneaking down to Wishworld. You don't want that . . . do you? If anyone found out, our lives would be ruined!"

Stella dropped Cora's hand and frowned at the thought of the trouble they would be in—but she couldn't let Starland remain in danger just to protect herself. "All I know is that we need to make sure somebody contains the negative energy before it does too much damage."

Cora shook her head and glanced back at the

Negative Energy Facility. "How much damage could that one cloud really do?" she asked before spinning around, challenging Stella with her eyes. "As much damage as confessing will do to us?"

Stella was torn. Starland was already in a positive energy drought, so any amount of negative energy would only make the situation worse. She felt her stomach drop with dread as she pondered how they could possibly safeguard Starland without endangering themselves—but then she had a moment of clarity. "Hey! Maybe we could report it anonymously!"

"No," Cora insisted, shaking her head more fervently than ever. "Please. We can't."

But the more Stella thought about it, the more it seemed like the best option. They could say there had been a negative energy leak without revealing anything about how it had happened. That way they could make sure it would be contained but nobody would have to find out about Cora's involvement, let alone their unlawful trip to Wishworld—especially now that Cora had destroyed the Bad Wish Orb. It was the perfect solution, albeit one that Stella might have to ease Cora into accepting.

"Well, we don't have to decide right this starsec," Stella told her friend, glancing around and taking a few steps along the path. "But we do need to get out of this place. It's giving me the creeps."

"Yeah," Cora agreed, "and if you think it's creepy out here, you should have seen what it was like inside."

"Ugh." Stella shook her head at her friend, amazed once again by how brave she'd been. "I'm not sure I even want to know."

The longer they walked and the more Cora talked about everything she'd done to destroy the Bad Wish Orb, the more optimistic Stella became. She even began to accept that perhaps the negative energy that had escaped wasn't significant enough to do any damage. She could feel the positive energy starting to reinvigorate her as she breathed in the fresh, clean air and the sky grew light enough to blend with the stars. Before long, the majestic peaks of the Crystal Mountains came into view in the distance, and by the time they reached Constellation Lane and the tall, swirly iron gates at the front of Starling Academy, Stella was all but convinced that the worst was behind them—literally.

"We're going to be all right," Stella whispered to Cora when they finally made it safely back inside their dorm room and the door slid closed. "*Everything's* going to be all right."

"I think so, too," Cora said with a big yawn, stretching out her arms and collapsing onto her bed.

But Stella didn't think so; she knew so—and she also knew that it was mostly thanks to Cora.

10

A faint buzzing sound roused Cora from sleep. Barely pushing back the covers, she swatted at her bedside table until her fingers landed on her Star-Zap. Finally, her eyes beginning to open, she sat up, raised the antenna, and peered at the screen. It was a holo-text from Lady Astrid, headmistress of Starling Academy: PLEASE REPORT TO MY OFFICE IMMEDIATELY.

That woke her up. But—wait, what? Lady Astrid's office? What time was it? What *day* was it?

Cora looked at the little clock on the Star-Zap screen. It was nearly lightfall. Had she really slept all day—and missed all her classes? Slowly, bits and pieces of the previous night and early morning filtered through her mind: the trip with Stella to Wishworld . . . Amy's bad wish . . . going to the Negative Energy Facility . . . successfully destroying the Bad Wish Orb!

Cora jumped out of bed and rushed up the steps to get Stella. But she wasn't there. Where could she be? Cora punched the Friend Finder button on her Star-Zap. There she was—already in Lady Astrid's office! What was going on?

Still dressed in the navy-blue leggings and long sweater she had been wearing when she fell asleep, Cora pulled on her boots and quickly used her toothlight. With no time for a sparkle shower, she hastily splashed some sparkler on her face and was about to rush out the door when she felt something jabbing into her side.

Cora shoved a hand into the right pocket of her sweater and discovered the black rock she'd picked up from the Negative Energy Facility—the one she'd used to prop the door open. Her fingers wrapped around its rough surface and she held it up, examining the sparkly threads of amethyst. It had a mesmerizing sort of dark beauty to it, and as she continued to turn it over in her hands, she began to feel the same surge of power she had felt before, when she was leaving the Negative Energy Facility.

Not knowing what to do with the rock, Cora placed it back in her pocket and headed for the Cosmic Transporter that would take her to Lady Astrid's office. She was about to knock on the headmistress's door, but before she got a chance, the gleaming silver panel slid open. She squared her shoulders and stepped inside.

There was Lady Astrid sitting behind her large gold desk—and there was Stella sitting in a comfy purple chair off to one side, although she looked anything but comfortable.

"Hello, Cora." The headmistress looked especially regal in a long, sparkling purple gown with a high gold collar. Her lavender hair was piled high atop her head and adorned with spirals of gold thread from which tiny stars dangled in a rainbow of bright colors.

"Hello, Lady Astrid," Cora replied, her voice slightly raspy from sleep. She glanced at Stella, hoping that her best friend might be able to give her some sort of silent clue as to what they were both doing there. But Stella was staring down at the glittery gold rug with the giant purple star in the center, clearly not wanting to meet Cora's gaze. *So be it,* Cora thought. She felt confident enough for them both.

"Please, have a seat." The headmistress gestured toward the other purple chair, pulled up at the opposite end of her desk from Stella's.

"Thank you," Cora replied with a bright smile as she sat in the chair, which immediately adjusted to her size and weight.

"How are you feeling?" the headmistress asked, leaning over her desk and narrowing her eyes as she scanned Cora from the top of her head to the toes of her boots.

"I'm feeling quite well, thank you." Cora cleared her throat and wondered if she was in trouble for missing classes that day. Maybe Stella had missed hers, too. On second thought, if she had, she would have still been in the dorm room when Cora was summoned.

"I see." Lady Astrid nodded. "Well, Stella is quite worried about you."

"She is?" Cora glanced at her friend again, but Stella continued to stare at the rug, her forehead wrinkled with worry.

"Yes." The headmistress drew in her breath and slowly blinked her eyes before looking more intently at Cora. "I'm quite worried, as well."

"I'm sorry—I don't understand," Cora replied, hoping Lady Astrid would cut to the chase.

"Well, from what *I* understand," Lady Astrid began, "you had quite an adventure last night."

What? Cora shot yet another look at Stella. Had the headmistress found out about their trip to Wishworld—or even about what had happened at the Negative Energy Facility? How would Lady Astrid have gotten the information? There was no way Stella would have told her, especially after she and Cora had agreed that it wasn't a big deal and they didn't need to report it. Or would she . . . ?

"I'm sorry?" Cora blinked a few times and then

widened her eyes, channeling all her acting skills in an attempt to appear as oblivious as possible.

"Cora," Lady Astrid said sternly, leaning back in her throne-like chair and crossing her arms, "I'm going to offer you a chance to tell me what happened."

"But—" Cora's heartbeat quickened and she shoved her hands into her pockets, only to discover the black rock once again. As her fingers touched the jagged surface, she instantly sat up taller, more self-assured than ever. "I don't know what you mean."

Cora focused all her energy on Stella, willing Stella to look at her. Finally, her friend's eyes drifted up, and Cora could see the pain, the fear, and especially the guilt in them.

Oh, my stars—did you tell her? Cora silently demanded—but Stella simply sighed and shifted her gaze back to the rug.

"Please," the headmistress said. "This is your opportunity to come clean—and I strongly suggest that you take it."

Cora frowned. She couldn't see any reason to admit to anything until Lady Astrid revealed what she knew. So she simply shrugged and stared blankly ahead.

"Well, that is too bad." The headmistress wrapped her long, elegant fingers around the golden scepter on her desk and stood up. As she rose, she seemed to grow to three times her usual size, while her eyes narrowed so much that they nearly disappeared. "Then I suppose I will have to be the one to tell *you* what happened."

Cora nodded and steeled herself as Lady Astrid revealed what she knew—which turned out to be every last detail, from Cora and Stella's sneaking down to Wishworld to their influencing Amy's bad wish, from Cora's going to the Negative Energy Facility to her breaking the Bad Wish Orb and releasing the cloud of negative energy. Each time she recounted a bit of evidence, she waved her scepter, and the gleaming light in her office dimmed ever so slightly while the ground shuddered.

"Am I missing anything?" the headmistress inquired, sinking back into her chair and setting down her scepter, when she'd reached the end of Cora and Stella's adventures.

In spite of all the charges she appeared to be facing, Cora felt certain she could help Lady Astrid understand that there was no reason to worry. She knew that just as she had convinced Stella that everything would be all right, she could convince the headmistress. After all, it seemed that Stella had made things out to be a bit less noble than they in fact were.

"When we went to Wishworld, it was with the best possible intentions," Cora began. "Stella and I had similar ideas for solving the drought on Starland, and Professor Shannon thought they were so good that she encouraged us to explore them—but we thought instead of doing the research in a practice Wish Orb, it might be a good idea to try an experiment with real Wishlings." Of course, it wasn't the *exact* reason they had made the journey—but the details were close enough and seemed reasonable and important enough to include.

"Indeed." Lady Astrid's face softened slightly. "Please tell me more about these ideas of yours."

"Of course," Cora agreed with a nod. "We wanted to help encourage Wishlings who have given up hope to start making good wishes again. The plan was to explore Wishworld a bit and figure out the best way to get them to believe in themselves, to realize their inner power and potential. If we could get them to do that, we thought it might help to restore the positive energy levels on Starland."

"Hmmm." The headmistress rose to her feet again and began pacing back and forth along the far wall of her office, which was lined with shelves of old holo-books. Finally, she returned to her chair and looked into Cora's eyes. "I do agree with Professor Shannon. Your ideas do have incredible merit and they show tremendous promise."

Cora brightened and she looked at Stella, who

offered a weak smile in return. But Stella had nothing to worry about. Thanks to Cora's explanation, they were both going to be all right. Cora was certain of it.

"But not only did you violate Starland's laws of Wishworld visitation, you chose to put yourself and all of Starland in danger," the headmistress added gravely.

Cora leaned back, startled by such accusations. "But we were trying to find a way to solve the drought," she pointed out. "We were trying to *help*."

"Understood," Lady Astrid replied. "But instead, you may have done the precise opposite—breaking yet another law by tampering with a Bad Wish Orb *and* releasing negative energy that we may never be able to contain!"

Cora shook her head and tried not to smirk. She almost felt sorry for the headmistress. Why was she making such a big deal out of something so small? "Truly, Lady Astrid, the amount of negative energy that escaped was hardly significant," she insisted. "I'd be surprised if it could even be detected in the Starland atmosphere at this point."

"Ah, but that's where you're wrong," Lady Astrid fired back, no longer the picture of composure. "Perhaps you failed to see the starveillance glameras outside of the Negative Energy Facility?"

Cora widened her eyes and sucked in her breath,

searching her mind as she thought back to what the facility had looked like. That was indeed news to her. Was Lady Astrid bluffing? "No," Cora said. "I didn't see any glameras."

"Interesting." Lady Astrid shot a stern look at Cora. "They're all around the entrance—so even if Stella hadn't come to me with the information that she did, the authorities most certainly would have."

"I see." Cora pressed her lips together but remained unruffled. "But were there glameras inside? Didn't the authorities see that I successfully destroyed the Bad Wish Orb?"

Lady Astrid shook her head. "Because everything on Starland must be powered by positive energy, there is no way to monitor activities *inside* the Negative Energy Facility," she explained, much to Cora's delight. "However, I can assure you that we *did* see an incredible amount of negative energy escape—a far from insignificant amount, as you claim—and it's going to take quite a lot of effort for the authorities to contain it before it does serious damage to Starland."

"Hmmm." As bad as the situation seemed, Cora remained certain that the headmistress was blowing things a bit out of proportion.

"'Hmmm'?" Lady Astrid retorted, slamming her

hands on her desk as she spun more wildly out of control. "That's all you have to say for yourself? The Negative Energy Facility was specifically designed to ensure that all Bad Wish Orbs would be contained—their toxic power never to be accessed or released—and you are responsible for violating that!"

Cora sighed. "Well, all I can tell you—again—is that my intentions were pure and good. I never intended for anything bad to happen."

Lady Astrid began to swirl her fingertips along the surface of her desk, as if she was looking into some sort of crystal ball. She closed her eyes and took several deep breaths. Then, at last, she spoke: "That may be. But regardless of intent, actions do have consequences—and the consequences of yours will be quite dire."

Cora blinked at the headmistress. She was really losing it.

"Because of your many violations," Lady Astrid continued, "and especially because of your decision to keep quiet when I offered you the opportunity to confess, I'm afraid that I'm going to be forced to expel you."

The only sound louder than Cora's gasp was Stella's shouting "No!"

"Both of us?" Cora demanded, shooting a look at her friend. "I mean—is Stella expelled, too?"

"Absolutely not," Lady Astrid replied firmly. "Stella put Starland's best interests above her own and reported the situation, so I've decided to grant her a reprieve."

"What?" Cora's eyes widened with rage and her heart beat in double time at the injustice of the situation. Anger surged through her like an electric shock.

How could Lady Astrid expel her? And how could Stella go free? Suddenly, it became clear to Cora: Stella must have known what would happen if she went to Lady Astrid like she did. Perhaps that was why she had done it—so she could clear her own name while destroying Cora's. She had thrown Cora under the starbus so that Cora would be the one to pay for everything, while Stella went free!

"I am truly sorry, Cora," the headmistress concluded. "However, you really left me no choice. Please return to your room and pack up your belongings. In the meantime, I will call your parents and make arrangements for your removal from Starling Academy."

So that was it? The final verdict? Cora was to be kicked out of school, and just a short time before she was supposed to graduate? As she narrowed her eyes at the headmistress, she could see that Lady Astrid's mind was made up. There was nothing she could do.

Cora slowly got to her feet. As she stood up and turned toward the door, she could feel Stella's eyes burning into her, silently begging her to look back—but Cora never wanted to look upon the face of her betrayer again. Being expelled meant not only that she would have to give up her leading role in the school's performance and leave her life there behind, but also that she wouldn't graduate and become a Wish-Granter! She couldn't believe it was happening.

As Cora headed out into the hallway and made her way past her classmates on the Cosmic Transporter, all of them oblivious to what had happened, she clutched the rock in her pocket and once again felt a jolt of power, like the one she had felt inside the NEF—but this time, it was all-consuming, unlike anything she'd felt before. A sense of supreme anger and righteousness was coursing through her veins and completely blackening her heart. It served to reinforce a growing certainty deep within her that she would find a way to make Stella and Lady Astrid pay. Oh, yes, they were most definitely going to regret this!

11

It had been three weeks since Cora was expelled from Starling Academy, and the dorm room Stella once shared with her best friend felt emptier than ever. She tried to focus on her studies, to carry on after everything that had happened, but it was a struggle—especially because Cora had refused to speak with her before her parents took her away, and she wouldn't accept any of Stella's repeated holo-calls, let alone respond to her holo-texts. Of course, Stella couldn't exactly blame her. Stella was the one who had gone to Lady Astrid to tell her about the accident at the Negative Energy Facility, after all. Even though it would have been discovered eventually, thanks to the starveillance glameras, Stella still couldn't help feeling that she was to blame for Cora's getting expelled.

She had genuinely intended to let the whole thing go, as she and Cora had discussed. But Cora had been asleep for so long after they'd returned from the Negative Energy Facility—she hadn't even gone to any of her classes that day!—and Stella couldn't stop thinking about that cloud of negative energy. She had desperately tried one last time to rouse Cora from sleep, hoping to convince her that reporting the leak would be the right thing to do, but Cora was in such a deep slumber that waking her had proved impossible. Fearing that it would soon be too late to contain the negative energy, and that it might endanger Starland, Stella felt she had no choice but to report it to Lady Astrid without Cora. Once the headmistress confirmed the details of the negative energy leak by accessing the starveillance footage, Stella felt that she had to confess to all the events leading up to that moment, as well, including her unauthorized trip down to Wishworld with Cora.

Stella knew that she and Cora would both get in trouble, but she never expected that Cora would be expelled! If only Cora had confessed when Lady Astrid had given her the chance, perhaps she would still be there at Starling Academy. But now she was gone. Cora had been right: their lives, or at least Cora's life, appeared to be ruined.

Stella shook her head and collapsed in tears on Cora's bed as all the plans they'd made began to flood her mind. They were supposed to graduate together. They were going to get their dream jobs—hers as a wish scientist and Cora's as an actor—and live next door to each other. And they would go on wish-granting missions together. But now the perfect future they'd envisioned seemed completely out of reach and Stella had never felt more alone. She buried her face in Cora's pillow, which still had a lingering hint of her best friend's sparkle-scent, and continued to sob. What if she never got to see her best friend again? *No!* There *had* to be a way to make things right—but it would require Lady Astrid's help. So Stella slowly got up from the bed and wiped away her tears—and within a few minutes, she was knocking at the door to the headmistress's office.

"Come in!" said Lady Astrid as the silver door slid open. "Stella—how nice to see you. I've been meaning to check on you, but things have been quite busy around here."

"Oh, that's okay," Stella replied with a pained smile.

"Please have a seat," Lady Astrid commanded, extending her arm in a grand gesture toward the same purple chair where Stella had sat a few weeks earlier. "What can I do for you?"

"Well," Stella began, "I was wondering if you'd heard anything about Cora—if you knew how she was doing."

"Ah." The headmistress nodded and drew in her breath. "I haven't been able to get ahold of her parents, but I'm sure they would have contacted me if there was a problem."

"Oh, that's good." Stella was relieved to hear that and felt her friend must be okay. When Cora hadn't taken any of her holo-calls or responded to her holo-texts, a small part of Stella worried that something awful had happened to her—although she of course realized it probably had more to do with Cora's being angry with her. "And the negative energy that escaped from the facility? Do you know what happened to it?"

"Yes," Lady Astrid replied with a comforting smile. "The Counter-Negative Unit was called in and they did indeed manage to capture and contain it."

"Really? That's wonderful!" Stella felt the weight of everything that had happened began to lift. Now she was more certain than ever that she could enlist Lady Astrid's help in making things right with Cora. "So are you going to let Cora come back to school?"

The headmistress widened her eyes in shock. "Oh, dear—no. I'm afraid that won't be possible."

"But why not?" Stella frowned. "Please, Lady Astrid! Cora is one of the kindest and most generous Starlings I've ever known—and she was truly trying to help! Everything she did came from the most positive place."

Lady Astrid's face softened with sympathy. "I know

it may seem that way to you, and accidents certainly do happen—but it is how we respond to those accidents that shows our true nature," the headmistress explained. "Unfortunately, one might argue that all of Cora's actions were in fact quite selfish, as noble as she may have believed her intentions to be—and at the very least, much of what she did following each mistake was motivated by a selfish desire to protect herself rather than others. That was clearly demonstrated when I offered her the chance to confess and she didn't take it."

It seemed like there was no way Lady Astrid was going to change her mind. Stella stared down at the purple star in the center of the sparkly gold rug and blinked back her tears. She wished Cora had just been honest about what had happened, and didn't understand why her friend had been so cold and distant when Lady Astrid called her into the office.

"However," the headmistress continued, "I must say that I am more impressed with you than ever before. Not only did you take a risk by coming to tell me what happened at the Negative Energy Facility and during your trip to Wishworld, but you continue to put others before yourself, as demonstrated by your efforts to help Cora yet again. You are a truly special girl, Stella. I hope you know that."

Stella inhaled deeply and struggled to smile through

her tears. The kind words from Lady Astrid should have made her feel at least a bit better, but instead they made her head throb with the same intense, painful guilt that had plagued her ever since Cora had been expelled. But then it occurred to her that if Lady Astrid held Stella in such high regard, there had to be some way for her to get through to the headmistress, to make her see how desperately Stella needed her best friend back.

"Thank you, Lady Astrid," she replied before attempting one final plea. "But I still can't help feeling like I was at least partly to blame for some of what happened, and I'm not sure how I'm ever going to live with myself if I can't find a way to reach Cora and get her to forgive me. Please—isn't there *anything* you can do?"

The headmistress shook her head sadly and pressed her hands together as she brought her fingertips to her lips, briefly closing her eyes before staring directly into Stella's. "I wish that I could," she said. "But it's quite simply out of my hands—and I suppose the time has come for me to tell you why. However, what I'm about to reveal must be held in the strictest of confidence and not shared with anyone. Especially Cora."

Stella felt like she'd been punched in the stomach, the breath knocked out of her completely. What could Lady Astrid possibly want to tell her, and why couldn't Cora know about it?

"Okay . . ." she barely managed to whisper.

"You see, Stella, I recently happened upon an oracle—an ancient text that spoke of the first time negative energy would be released into the Starland atmosphere," the headmistress said.

"Oh, my goodness—you did?" Stella gasped.

"Yes," Lady Astrid replied with a contemplative smile. "In fact, the prophecy specifically said that two Starlings would take a forbidden trip to Wishworld, and that the negative energy would be released as a result of that journey."

Stella's head continued to throb as she tried to process what the headmistress was telling her. It was almost impossible to believe. How could it be that everything she and Cora had done had been foretold—that their journey to Wishworld had already been written in the stars and they had simply been fulfilling their destinies?

"However," Lady Astrid continued, "the oracle also stated that only one of the Starlings would be responsible for the release of the negative energy, while the other would be responsible for stopping its spread—in effect, for saving Starland."

"Really?" Stella replied, her eyes widening with a mix of fear and reluctant pride as the magnitude of her part in the prophecy sunk in. "It said that?"

"It did." The headmistress nodded.

"I see." Stella swallowed hard and pressed her lips together to stop them from trembling.

"Now that Cora has been stopped and the negative energy has been contained, I cannot possibly allow her to return to Starling Academy," Lady Astrid said. "To do so would directly undermine the prophecy—and truly, given all of her offenses, I believe that she is in fact getting off quite easy. Do you understand?"

"I think so," Stella replied.

"Good," Lady Astrid concluded.

But Stella didn't see anything good about it. All she knew was that she needed to take some time to think about everything she'd just learned. It still didn't seem fair that she got to stay at Starling Academy while Cora had to be expelled, and although she realized that she had to do as Lady Astrid said and keep what she'd just learned in confidence, she remained convinced that she needed to find a way to reach Cora—to somehow make things right between the two of them. Because no matter what the ancient oracle had predicted and no matter how different their destinies might appear to be in that moment, Stella refused to accept that she had lost her best friend forever. If there was any way for her to somehow realign their stars, she would find it.

12

Feeling a bit dazed after her conversation with Lady Astrid, Stella slowly made her way out of Halo Hall and headed down the path that led to the serene banks of Luminous Lake. Once there, she sat at the picnic table where she and Cora had been together just a few short weeks earlier—when Cora had proven to be the best friend ever by throwing a surprise Bright Day party for her. It was the perfect spot for Stella to try to reach out to Cora, to tell her once again how much she appreciated her—and how much she missed and needed to be back in touch with her.

Stella took a few deep breaths and then, with trembling hands, made the holo-call. One ring . . . two rings . . . three rings . . . four. As usual, it went to Cora's message center; but this time, instead of ending the call, and instead of briefly asking Cora to call her back, Stella left a much longer holo-message.

"Hi, Cora, it's me—Stella," she began, her voice shaking. Then the words began tumbling out of her mouth at top speed: "I know you've probably seen that I've been calling you, and I'm sure you've received all my holo-messages and holo-texts, too, and I also know how angry you must be with me for reporting what happened to Lady Astrid—and you have every reason to blame me and hate me for it.

"But, Cora, please, you have to believe me—I tried to wake you up so we could report the incident together! I was just so worried about that negative energy leak. I never meant for you to get expelled and I miss you so much it hurts! You're the best friend I've ever had and I can't lose you. Please just call me back. I'm begging you! If you can somehow find it in your heart to forgive me, I know that we can get past this. I just know it!"

Stella paused for a moment and cleared her throat, unsure of what else she could possibly say. "Okay, then . . . um . . . bye."

The moment Stella pressed the End button and lowered the antenna, she burst into tears again. At least she'd gotten it all out this time, and she could only hope it would be enough to get Cora to respond. But Stella also knew that it might not be enough—that she might never hear her friend's voice, or see her face, again. What more could she do, though? She stared down at the screen of her Star-Zap, mustering every bit of positive energy she could, silently begging Cora to call back, willing the Star-Zap to ring.

But no amount of energy manipulation would be enough. Stella knew that. So she wiped the tears from her eyes, stood up, and walked down to the edge of the lake. Looking out at the smooth azure surface, she suddenly had the urge to throw her Star-Zap into the water so she wouldn't have to stand there waiting, wondering if Cora would ever reply. Instead, she put the Star-Zap back in the pocket of her pink skirt and sat down on the soft grass.

Staring across the lake, she could see Star Prep off in the distance, and it made her wonder what Ozzie and Theo were up to. Had Theo heard from Cora since she'd been expelled? Perhaps Stella could call him or at least find out from Ozzie—and then maybe Theo could get Cora to call her back. Yes! Why hadn't she thought of that before? It was definitely worth a try!

Stella pulled the Star-Zap out of her pocket and was about to press Ozzie's number when a holo-text came through. It was from Cora! At last! She had finally responded! Stella touched her finger to the message, barely able to contain her nervous excitement as the words floated up before her eyes and she realized how long the message was. Stella assumed that that was a good thing, but of course she didn't need to assume anymore—she simply needed to read it.

Stella: I got your holo-text—and all your other messages. I'm amazed that you actually said more than ten words this time—not that I believed a single one of them. At least you managed to get a few things right, though: 1) Yes, I am BEYOND angry that you reported everything to Lady Astrid. 2) Yes, I do blame you and hate you for it. 3) You were definitely responsible for some of what happened—you broke rules by going down to Wishworld, too! I was the one who tried to fix everything. I was the one who got rid of the Bad Wish Orb! And what thanks did I get? None. Instead I got EXPELLED. And yet you didn't—even though you should have been.

So now you get to stay at Starling Academy and then graduate and go on to get the future and life you want (and probably even the job you want, if you're still planning to steal my ideas for the Wish-Science Fair!). Meanwhile, I'm supposed to be shipped off to a brighting facility, where I'll basically be turned into a Bot-Bot who can't think for herself, who does everything by the holo-book. My dream of an acting career couldn't seem further away. As if that weren't enough, Theo broke up with me and my parents and my brother are so disappointed in me that they act like they don't even know me anymore. I have never felt so misjudged, unfairly punished, rejected, and alone.

But the truth is that I don't need them, and I most definitely don't need you!!! As far as I'm concerned, you have already completed your Cycle of Life. So no matter how much you might beg and plead for my forgiveness, I can't hear you anymore. I won't hear you. Because I'M NOT LISTENING! So please stop holo-calling me and stop holo-texting me. It won't do you any good from this day forward, because I'm going to block you from my contacts. We are no longer friends and we never will be again. Good-bye and good riddance!!!

Stella could barely let out a breath as she sat there, staring at the holo-text for so long that the message became nothing but a blur. But she could hear Cora's awful words echoing in her head, making it throb more painfully than ever before. How could she have said such things, no matter how angry she was feeling—and how could she cut Stella off completely, with no way to reach her ever again? It was more than Stella could bear. She desperately searched her mind for another solution, but it was a complete blank. She was out of options.

Finally, after what felt like an eternity, Stella closed her Star-Zap, got up from the grass, and trudged back to the room she once shared with Cora. As hurt as she was by everything that had been said, she couldn't be angry or even sad anymore. All she felt was numb, and all she could do was silently wish that one day Cora might find it in her heart to forgive her. As much as Stella wanted to take action, to do something to change the situation, she knew she would have to accept that it was entirely beyond her control—for the moment, anyway. Maybe it always had been.

As her final weeks at Starling Academy drew to a close, Stella refocused all of her energy on her studies. Anytime she thought about Cora, she channeled the memory into something positive—particularly when it came to her Wish-Science Fair project. As she toiled away in the lab, working inside one practice Wish Orb after another, she succeeded in proving her theory beyond any shadow of a doubt: while granting practice wishes, she was able to encourage Wishling girls to believe in themselves!

Then, each time a girl's hope was restored, the most magical thing happened, just as Stella had presented it in Wishworld Relations class that day: a Good Wish Orb materialized and went zooming up to Starland. Even though it was only practice, and even though a small part of her couldn't shake Cora's accusations about her stealing the idea, it was still the most wonderful feeling

Stella had ever experienced, and she couldn't wait for the day she would get the chance to try to make it happen for real.

But when graduation day finally arrived, Stella got a sinking sense that a dark cloud was following her around. She wanted so much to focus on all the great things to come—such as her galactictorian address presentation! Receiving her Wish-Granting degree! And learning how she had fared at the Wish-Science Fair; maybe, just maybe, she had won! But while pulling on her long, sparkly golden robe and then placing the gold star-shaped graduation cap on her head, she glanced back at her dorm room on the way out the door. It was then a wave of sadness and guilt washed over her. She was almost certain that she could hear Cora's voice telling her that she didn't deserve to be there, that she should have been expelled, too. Terrified, Stella rushed to meet up with the rest of her classmates, hoping the menacing voice she was hearing in her head wouldn't persist.

Thankfully, when she joined the long line of girls filing into the Radiant Recreation Center, Stella heard instead three sweet little voices laughing and calling out her name in unison. She turned in time to see her younger sisters waving to her. She felt a positive glow as she waved back, and pure joy overtook her when she locked eyes with her parents, who were beaming back at her with pride. Yes, this was what she needed to focus on—the positive energy was all around her. She just needed to remain focused on it.

Everything that happened after that—including Stella's own galactictorian address—was a blur. All she wanted to do was find out who had won first place in the Wish-Science Fair! At long last, it was time, and she could hardly contain her excitement as Lady Astrid walked to the front of the stage and began talking about the significance of that year's projects. Stella glanced around at her classmates but avoided making eye contact with any of them and instead looked over at her parents and her sisters again—five sparkling pairs of eyes all smiling back at her, filling her up with the confidence she so desperately needed. They believed in her, so how could she help believing in herself?

"And so, without further ado," Lady Astrid said, "in third place . . . please give your most cosmic congratulations to . . . Indirra Solara!"

As she watched Indirra walk along the glittery silver path up to the stage, Stella smiled and clapped as loudly as she could—but self-doubt and fear began to creep in. If Indirra had come in third, did that mean Stella might only come in second? After all, Stella usually came in first with Indirra just behind her. She shook her head, trying to push aside the negative voices; a hush fell over the crowd as the headmistress prepared to read the name of the second-place finisher.

"Next," said Lady Astrid, "in second place . . . congratulations to . . . Marisol Meriwether!"

Oh, my stars! Stella couldn't believe it. Marisol was only a second-year student! Was that a good thing . . . or a bad thing? It was hard to say. Slowly, Stella turned around in her seat to look at her family, and once again she saw their bright faces smiling back at her. It didn't matter to them if she won the Wish-Science Fair. To them, she was already a star. Stella smiled and looked up at Lady Astrid. She took a deep breath and reminded herself that the judges had already made their decision and she simply had to hope for the best. As the cheers died down again, Stella squeezed her eyes shut and held her breath.

"And now, it is my distinct honor and privilege to not only award first place, but to join with the heads of the Starland Wish-Tank in offering a most coveted position to . . ."

Just then, a Bad Wish Orb zoomed over the stage, nearly striking Lady Astrid in the head, before making its way through the crowd. Stella felt sick as it came right up to her, buzzing angrily, before finally shooting off into the atmosphere and—thank the stars—disappearing.

"Well, that was most unusual," said Lady Astrid, who appeared shaken but then quickly cleared her throat and regained her composure. "As I was saying . . . the award for first place goes to . . ."

Stella tried hard to focus on Lady Astrid, but the Bad Wish Orb's buzzing was still echoing in her ears, so loud that she couldn't hear what the headmistress was saying. Had she announced the winner? She saw Lady Astrid's lips moving but couldn't make out the name she was citing. Stella glanced around, and as the stadium erupted in thunderous applause, it finally registered that all eyes were on her. She turned to look at her parents, who were nodding and cheering and motioning for her to go up to the stage.

"Me?" asked Stella as she blinked a few times, and they responded by nodding more urgently while laughing happily.

Stella wanted to laugh, too—but she also wanted to cry. She felt completely disoriented as she raced up to the stage and did her best to thank a woman named Skylar, who would soon be her mentor at the Starland Wish-Tank. Skylar shook Stella's hand and congratulated her. Then, at last, Lady Astrid extended her arms and Stella nearly collapsed into them as she returned her embrace. When they broke apart, Stella looked out at the crowd— her classmates, their families, *her* family—and tried to enjoy the moment.

But as Stella thought about the dark cloud that had been hanging over her all day, not to mention the Bad Wish Orb that had made such an ill-timed appearance, she had a strange and troubling sense that her victory might not last—that something terrible might be right around the corner. Was it possible that Lady Astrid was wrong—that Stella hadn't stopped the spread of negative energy after all, and perhaps she still had far more work to do? And worse than that, could it be that Cora still had something to do with it?

PRESENT-DAY STARLAND

All twelve Star Darlings stared in stunned silence at the staryearbook resting on Adora's lap, trying to process everything they had just seen.

"Oh. My. Stars," Adora finally said, her hand trembling as it hovered above the image of Stella on her graduation day. "Can you believe it?"

"Of course I can," Vega replied, grabbing the staryearbook. Her blue eyes sparkled with admiration as she considered everything their headmistress had accomplished when she was about their age. "It was so obvious that Lady Stella—er, I mean, just Stella—was going to win the Wish-Science Fair and go to work in the Wish-Tank."

"My mom did pretty well, too," Sage pointed out.

"Who cares about that?" Adora interjected impatiently. "Can we talk about how Rancora—as in *Cora*—is Lady Stella's best friend ... or at least *former* best friend?"

"Incredible!" Scarlet nodded while pacing back and forth in front of the plush orange couch. "It all makes sense now—no wonder she disguised herself as Lady Cordial and came to work at Starling Academy. She's been trying to bring down Lady Stella for getting her expelled—and that was totally her trying to ruin things at the graduation ceremony!"

Vega narrowed her blue eyes at Scarlet and then scrolled back to the image they had of their then young headmistress. She looked so accomplished, standing there in her golden star-shaped graduation cap. "But Lady Stella didn't mean for anything bad to happen to Cora," Vega pointed out. "She did everything she could to make things right—and Cora would have been expelled anyway, once Lady Astrid saw the starveillance footage. Plus, like Lady Astrid said, her punishment could have been a lot worse!"

"But Cora couldn't see that," sighed Libby with tears in her eyes. "Why couldn't she just forgive Stella?"

"Isn't it obvious?" Adora asked. "The oracle said Cora would be the one to release the negative energy, and Stella would be the one to stop it—so they were basically destined to be enemies!"

Scarlet walked over to Vega and grabbed the star-yearbook, scrolling it back until she accessed the angry holo-text Cora sent to Stella.

"Yes, but how did she turn from Cora to *Rancora*— and how did she release all the negative energy that led to the crisis we just stopped? That's what I want to know."

"Me too," agreed Adora. "I think she was affected by the cloud of negative energy inside the NEF. That and the rock she picked up in the Negative Energy Facility."

"But how did she collect so much negative energy?" Sage wondered.

"I don't know—that's what we need to find out," Adora replied.

"How are we going to do that?" asked Cassie, blinking nervously behind her star-shaped glasses.

"We need to go to the Negative Energy Facility," Adora proposed. "Maybe we can collect more of those black rocks and do some tests on them."

Vega gasped and shook her head. "No way—going to the Negative Energy Facility would be way too dangerous!"

"Don't worry about that," Adora replied. "I've got an idea that's both fashionable and functional!"

"Oh, really?" Vega demanded.

"Uh-huh." Adora nodded without wavering. "I'll design special protective suits for us to wear—kind of like the ones those Bad Wish Orb Gatherers were wearing when Cora snuck in. Believe it or not, I've been doing a lot of research in the lab ever since the negative energy crisis started, so I know exactly what materials I can use to make them."

Vega sighed but remained skeptical. "Yeah, right. Have you ever done any research using *real* negative energy—like from an actual Bad Wish Orb—before?"

"Well, no, but—"

"Exactly," Vega concluded.

But Sage felt reassured as she peered over Scarlet's shoulder at the staryearbook. "Actually . . . I think Adora might be right—I think we'll find out everything we need to know in the Negative Energy Facility."

"I do, too," Scarlet agreed, her eyes lighting up in eager anticipation. "I want to check that place out!"

"I'm telling you, it's way too dangerous," Vega insisted. "I say we go find out more about Lady Stella— like what happened after she went to work in the Wish-Tank."

"How would we do that?" Gemma asked.

"We can go to her office, where *The Great Holo-Book of Wish-Granters* is kept," Vega proposed. "The details of all of her Wish Missions will be there for sure."

Adora rolled her eyes. "How's that going to help?"

"We'll be able to see if she ever managed to encourage Wishlings to make more wishes—and maybe learn other techniques that Starlings in the Wish-Tank used to generate lots of positive wish energy," Vega reasoned.

"Especially if we wind up needing to solve this whole thing by going on more Wish Missions, it would be super helpful to see some of their trips down to Wishworld."

"You just think you'll find some information that will help you with your Wish-Science Fair project—but you're never going to beat me," Adora scoffed.

"Wrong." Vega frowned and crossed her arms, even though the thought of learning about Lady Stella and the Wish-Tank's missions did suddenly appeal to her a lot more than finding out how Rancora harnessed all of her negative energy.

Adora shrugged. "Okay, fine. If you want to check out *The Great Holo-Book,* go ahead—but I'm going to the Negative Energy Facility. It's the only way we're going to get the information we really need about Rancora."

"I agree," Piper chimed in as she strolled over to where Scarlet was standing with the staryearbook. "I'm getting a powerful feeling that we must go to the Negative Energy Facility—that it will hold all the answers."

Vega cringed at her roommate's ominous prediction. "Seriously?" she snapped at Piper. "How are you even going to get in? I guarantee you they changed the code on that lock and probably added a lot more security, too."

"I bet I can get MO-J4 to help us find a way," Sage offered, knowing how devoted and capable her close personal Starling Academy-appointed Bot-Bot guide would be.

"I still say it will never work," Vega said, tossing her short blue bob as she got up from the couch. "I'm going to Lady Stella's office. Whoever's with me is welcome to join."

"Go ahead," Adora replied, also standing up. "I'm going to make those suits, and anyone who wants to find out more about the source of all Rancora's negative energy—anyone who's not too scared, that is—can join *me*."

With that, Adora straightened the hem on her shimmering blue tunic and headed toward the winding staircase leading down to the first floor of the library.

"Sorry, but I'm going with Adora," Piper said softly to Vega, giving her roommate's shoulder a gentle squeeze before making her way to the staircase as well.

"Me too," said Sage—and then Astra nodded and followed as well.

"I did like those shiny yellow suits the Bad Wish Gatherers were wearing!" Leona added, also heading out.

"Yup—see ya!" Scarlet gave a quick salute to Vega and stomped over to the staircase.

Vega widened her bright blue eyes, astonished that

so many of the girls would do something so risky. "Well," she said, turning to search the faces of the remaining Star Darlings. "Are any of you coming with me?"

"I guess so," Gemma replied with a tentative nod.

"I don't know," said Cassie as she wrinkled her nose. "Don't you think we should try to stop Adora and the others? I'm really worried about them going to the Negative Energy Facility."

"Me too," said Tessa. "Adora's my roommate! Even if she makes those jumpsuits, what if the negative energy still winds up doing something to her, like it did to Cora, and then she tries to do something awful to me . . . or to all of us?"

"They've already made their decision—just like Cora made hers," Clover pointed out.

"She's right," agreed Libby. "I say we go to Lady Stella's office and find *The Great Holo-Book of Wish-Granters.*"

"Thank you, Libby. Anyone else?" Vega asked with a hopeful, inviting tone to her voice.

One by one, each of the girls finally agreed. Vega smiled gratefully and they all headed downstairs and out of the library. But once they arrived at the door to Lady Stella's office, Vega suddenly had second thoughts. What if the headmistress caught them? Could they be the ones who would wind up getting expelled like Cora had—even if they were trying to do the right thing and find a way to help?

"Are you sure about this, Vega?" Cassie asked, picking up on the growing nervous energy that they had carried in with them.

"I—I think so," Vega replied, trying to reassure herself as much as anyone else. "It's still early enough, so Lady Stella probably won't be here for a while...."

"But how do we get into her office?" Gemma whispered.

"Step aside," Tessa told her little sister, gently moving her out of the way. She then trained her bright emerald eyes on the gleaming silver door and used her energy manipulation skills to slide it open.

"Nicely done," Vega said, pushing past Tessa and leading the group inside.

Once there, the girls all gathered around the large silver table—the very one where they had first learned they had been chosen to be Star Darlings. Vega finally felt certain that they were doing the right thing.

"Do you know where Lady Stella keeps *The Great Holo-Book*?" Libby asked. As a first-year student, she hadn't even realized there was a place where they could look up all the Wish Missions that had taken place throughout Starland's history.

"Of course." Vega marched straight over to the far wall of the office, which was lined with shelves of old holo-books. Lady Stella occasionally loaned out some of them, but *The Great Holo-Book* was one that students typically could not borrow. Vega, however, had seen it on the shelf and thought she remembered where it was located. But when she got to the spot where she thought it would be, she couldn't find it. "*Hmmm*—that's weird. It's not here."

"Well, where else could it be?" Tessa asked, a little bewildered.

"I don't know." Vega frowned and began wandering around the office, running a finger along the spines of the holo-books as she studied each title. "Everyone start looking."

While most of the others followed Vega's lead and began looking through the shelves of the headmistress's holo-books, Gemma couldn't resist sitting down in Lady Stella's desk chair. "Star Darlings," she said in her most sophisticated voice, smoothing down her bright orange hair and elongating her spine as she attempted to impersonate the headmistress, "I am most impressed with your efforts to assist me with this crisis!"

"Cut it out, Gem," Tessa whispered, narrowing her green eyes so that they focused in on just her sister.

"Aw, you're no fun," Gemma replied, sticking out

her tongue before turning her gaze to one of the desk drawers and using her energy manipulation powers to open it. However, she did this a bit too forcefully, and its contents immediately flew up into the air.

"Oh, my stars!" Cassie gasped when she saw what Gemma had done. "You shouldn't be looking in there. Those are Lady Stella's private belongings!"

"Oops," Gemma said with an apologetic, if somewhat exaggerated, shrug. But as she began lowering everything back into the desk drawer, one of the objects caught her older sister's eye.

"Hey—is that Lady Stella's new energy meter?" Tessa asked, racing over to pluck a small round instrument out of the air. It was gold and had a circle in the center where an arrow would move between the words *good* and *bad*, reading the current level of energy.

"Oooh, it is!" Cassie hurried over to take a look at the meter, forgetting that she'd reprimanded Gemma only a moment earlier.

"Cool!" interjected Clover as she tipped up the rim on her purple hat and joined the others at Lady Stella's desk.

They all watched in awe as Tessa trained her eyes on the meter, not to use it for its intended function, but rather to make it bounce around in the air. But just then, it seemed to take on a life of its own. It started flying all around the office, weaving furiously as it zipped over the head of each girl.

"Yikes!" Cassie squealed when it skimmed over her pale pink pigtails and bumped her on the shoulder before heading in Vega's direction.

"Watch out!" Gemma shouted, warning Vega just in time. She ducked down just as the energy meter narrowly missed hitting her in the head.

Then, while still crouching, Vega focused her blue eyes upon the meter, using all of her strength to send it soaring back over to the desk and into the still-open drawer. "Stop messing around," she huffed at the girls with a final glare at the drawer, which promptly slammed shut. "We need to stay focused!"

"Sorry," Cassie replied, exchanging sheepish grins with Gemma, Tessa, and Clover as they turned their attention back to the bookshelves.

"Hey—I found it!" Libby suddenly called out, picking up a gleaming gold holo-book lying on a table near the expansive window that overlooked the Starling Academy campus.

"Let's see," Vega said, racing over to examine the tome. "Yes! That's it! Good work, Libby."

"Thanks," said Libby. She smiled and tossed her shiny pink hair proudly as everyone followed Vega over to Lady Stella's desk.

"Okay," Vega said, shooing Gemma out of the big desk chair and claiming it as her own while the rest of the girls gathered around. Her heart began to beat with nervous excitement as she scanned through the pages of *The Great Holo-Book*, searching for references to Lady Stella.

"There she is!" Tessa gasped when an image of their then young headmistress appeared. "I know the others want to find out about Rancora, but I think learning what happened to Stella at the Wish-Tank after she graduated is important, too."

"I agree," Vega said.

In the holo-photo, Lady Stella wore a silver lab coat and was sitting at a long glass conference table in a sparkling blue office. On the wall behind her, the words *Starland Wish-Tank* were spelled out in shiny gold letters. Beneath her image was a chart containing the records of every last one of her Wish Missions. At the top were several categories, including the dates of the mission, the name of the Wisher, and the amount of positive wish energy that had been generated.

"Hey, look at this," Vega said as she studied the chart and noticed that two of the Wish Missions on the list glowed more brightly than the rest, and that both had markings next to them that resembled an image of

Wishworld. "These two missions have an extra code of some sort."

"What do you think it means?" Gemma wondered.

"There's only one way to find out," Vega replied. "Ready?"

Without even waiting for a reply, Vega tapped on the first of the special links and drew in her breath as the details surrounding the Wish Mission were revealed. . . .

PART TWO

STELLA'S RISING STAR

13

As Stella sat in the Wish-Tank conference room, she couldn't believe she had just graduated Starling Academy two years earlier. Now she was part of the esteemed Wish-Tank, waiting for her colleagues to arrive and hear her presentations on the findings from her most recent Wish Mission. As she looked out the window, Stella suddenly was overcome by a strong sense that something big was about to happen. It was the same jolt of positive energy she had felt shortly after beginning her job there, when she first proposed what had officially become known as the Wish Motivation Protocol—an approach to Wish Missions that was largely based on the research used in her Wish-Science Fair project.

In the two staryears since the protocol had been put in place, Stella and the other Wish-Granters in the Wish-Tank had gone on countless Wish Missions, but with a new focus: to help encourage Wishling girls other than the primary Wisher to believe in themselves and make more good wishes.

Their missions had been hugely successful, ultimately resulting in an exponential rise in positive wish energy on Starland.

And the most recent assignment had been Stella's most successful to date, generating a full ten Good Wish Orbs from girls she had come into contact with while on her mission. It was the highest number anyone in the Wish-Tank had achieved—and Stella was eager to share her new insights with the team. She sat a bit taller in her chair as the other members of the Wish-Tank began entering the room, chatting happily with each other as they sipped from travel mugs full of hot Zing and took their seats. Then, at last, Skylar—the lead advisor in the group—arrived. Her hair fell like a long cape of yellow curls halfway down her back and she wore a glittery gold version of the standard silver lab coat worn by the rest of the Wish-Tank staff.

"Thank you for being here, everyone," Skylar said with a warm smile as she stood at the head of the glass conference table. "I know we were all expecting Stella to present the findings from her most recent Wish Mission today—and while I'm sure that she's eager to share the details, I'm afraid we're going to have to postpone her report for now. I need to speak to Stella first."

Almost immediately, all the positive energy that had been flowing in the room felt as if it had been sucked out. What could be more important than Stella's news about garnering ten new Good Wish Orbs from her last mission?

As if reading Stella's thoughts, Skylar said, "I'm sorry I can't tell you anything more for the moment— but I hope to be able to soon enough." She then turned to Lena, who had been working in the Wish-Tank for nearly eight staryears and, as a result, was the second-highest-ranking member of the group. "Lena, can you please lead the rest of the meeting?"

"Of course," Lena replied, adjusting the star-shaped clip in her cropped lavender hair.

"Stella," Skylar then said as she headed for the door. "Can you please come with me?"

Stella's concern increased. What was this about, exactly? Had something gone wrong on her last mission without Stella'a realizing it? She wasn't so sure she wanted to find out, but she didn't exactly have a choice— so she slowly rose to her feet and blinked a farewell to the rest of the Wish-Tank staff before following Skylar out of the conference room.

Once they were in the hallway, Skylar glanced over at Stella. "Oh, don't look so worried!" she said with a kind smile. "Come on—I have something extremely important to share with you."

The flutterfocuses in Stella's stomach settled down ever so slightly as Skylar led her through the shimmering blue corridors of the Wish-Tank building. A few moments later, they arrived at the gold door leading out to the Wishworld Launchpad, where Wish-Granters caught the shooting stars that took them on their Wish Missions.

"What's going on?" Stella asked, unable to take the suspense any longer.

"You'll see," Skylar replied as she placed her palm on the scanner next to the Launchpad door, prompting it to slide open.

Once outside, Stella followed Skylar across the sparkling blue deck and over to a short Launchpad worker with fiery orange hair sticking out of his head in all directions. As soon as he saw the Wish-Tank advisor, he reached into a silver cabinet and retrieved a glowing Wish Orb, which he carefully handed to Skylar.

"Stella," Skylar said, turning around and holding up the orb, which had an almost blinding aura, "I believe this Wish Orb presents a unique opportunity for you, and for the Wish-Tank—one that could take our Wish Motivation Protocol to an entirely new level."

Stella inhaled, and examined the surface of the orb. It swirled in shades of emerald, blue, and silver—almost like a replica of Wishworld itself. In the two staryears she'd been going on Wish Missions, she'd never seen one quite like it.

Stella was nearly speechless. "Really?"

"Yes." Skylar nodded solemnly. "I can't tell you much more, except to say that this is bound to be your most important—but also most challenging—Wish Mission yet."

Stella blinked as she stared up at her mentor, and the flutterfocuses returned to her stomach. But this time it was pure excitement rather than worry that was triggering the flutterfocuses—and the sense that something big was about to happen, just as she had speculated. Stella looked at the orb again as Skylar handed it to her.

"Are you ready?" she asked.

"I think so," Stella replied, holding the orb with both hands as she followed Skylar over to two Star Wranglers, who were waiting to attach her to a shooting star so she could make her trip down to Wishworld.

"Good luck!" Skylar called out to Stella once she was fastened to the star.

"Thank you!" Stella called back. With that, she was on her way.

She had been on enough Wish Missions at that point and was even used to the exhilarating journey experience down to Wishworld. But somehow this mission felt different. This time Stella was overcome with a thrilling anticipation unlike anything she had ever experienced—and she could hardly wait to see where this extra-special Wish Mission was about to take her.

14

As Stella approached the Wishworld atmosphere, she looked down at her Star-Zap and followed the familiar COMMENCE APPEARANCE CHANGE instructions, punching the Wishworld Outfit Selector button. She replaced her silver lab coat with a pink sweater and changed into a pair of cropped pants with white socks and sneakers. Then, holding tightly to the Wish Pendant hanging around her neck, she said, "Star light, star bright, the first star I see tonight: I wish I may, I wish I might, have the wish I wish tonight," prompting her long golden-pink hair to change to a plain light brown and her skin to lose its sparkly glow.

Stella could barely contain her excitement when the Star-Zap told her to prepare for landing and she touched down on a concrete path just outside of an enormous white building with a dark dome-shaped roof. She picked up the star that had brought her to Wishworld, folding it up and placing it in her pink handbag along with her safety glasses. She wanted to meet her Wisher right away, but she was also eager to explore her surroundings. Spinning around to take it all in, she realized she was high up on a hill with a view of the entire city down below, where tiny dots of light illuminated the buildings and appeared blurry along vast highways stretching in all directions.

The sun was beginning to set on the horizon, lighting up the sky in dazzling shades of lavender and pink. It was positively breathtaking!

She could have stood there for hours, mesmerized by the view, but Stella knew she needed to get to work. So she took out her Star-Zap and followed the directions, which indicated that she would find her Wisher on the other side of the building. After making her way past the many large telescopes, which were built into the low wall lining the path, she came to the front of the building and noticed that there were Wishlings all over the place who seemed to be as fascinated by the location as she was. Most of them were holding glameras—well, what Wishlings called cameras—and taking pictures of the building, as well as the city down below and the mountains off in the distance; many were biding their time, then taking turns looking through the telescopes.

Above the entrance to the building were black letters spelling out the words GRAFFIELD OBSERVATORY. There was also a sign next to the steps leading into the massive building's domed doorway, which stated ASTRONOMY FOR ALL. Stella stepped closer so she could read the rest of the sign, which talked about the history of the place. It said that the observatory was built to bring the stars and the planets to everyone because of the great desire people had to see them up close.

Stella shivered in excitement as the words sunk in; this place was almost exactly like the Wishworld Surveillance Decks on Starland, only in reverse!

There was so much more Stella wanted to learn about this fascinating place, but she noticed her Star-Zap lighting up and silently scolded herself for taking so long to get to her Wisher. So she continued along the path until she came to the side of the building, where she saw a paper sign on a wooden post stuck into the grassy hill. In large block letters, the sign said YOUNG SCIENTISTS LUNAR ECLIPSE PARTY! FRIDAY, MAY 3. COME ONE, COME ALL!

Just beyond the sign, Stella saw a girl setting up some sort of equipment. A bit farther away, there was a boy putting together a similar apparatus, and then another boy, and even another. As Stella walked toward the girl, she looked down at the Wish Pendant hanging around her neck. The closer she got, the more brightly the pink orb glowed. Yes, this was definitely her Wisher.

"Hello," Stella said when she got close enough.

The girl turned around and smiled when she saw Stella. She had light brown hair pulled into two pigtails and wore a yellow-and-pink argyle sweater with a pair of cropped pink pants similar to Stella's.

"Hi." The girl wrinkled her nose and narrowed her brown eyes at Stella. "You're not here for the lunar eclipse party, are you?"

"I actually am," said Stella while nodding.

The girl looked positively thrilled, if a bit surprised. "Really?" she asked. "Another girl! Finally!"

"Yeah." Stella quickly caught on to the situation. "None of my other friends were interested in joining me, so I had to come by myself."

"Same here," the girl replied with a slight frown as she extended her arm. "I'm Lindie."

"Nice to meet you," Stella said, reaching out to shake Lindie's hand. "I'm Stella."

"Nice to meet you, too." Lindie tilted her head and narrowed her eyes again. "Did you bring a telescope?"

A *telescope!* That must be what Lindie and the boys were setting up—but the large, boxy equipment looked nothing like the sleek high-powered ones used on Starland, nor the ones along the path of the observatory.

"No." Stella shook her head, appearing disappointed. "I was hoping someone here might be willing to share."

"I'd be happy to!" answered Lindie, who became so excited she looked like she might actually lose her balance and go tumbling down the hill. "I just finished building this one last night."

"You *built* this?" Stella stared at the collection of silver cylinders, rods, and boxes.

Lindie beamed. "Yup. It's almost ready." She turned around and began connecting the parts again while Stella watched.

Meanwhile, the sky was growing dark and more people, mostly boys about the same age as Lindie, along with a few younger Wishlings and their parents, arrived and set up their own telescopes. Before long, the moon—a bright and full one this night—shone high above them, and tiny dots of light appeared all over the night sky. Stella drew in her breath as she gazed up.

"Isn't it wonderful?" Lindie sighed.

"It is," Stella agreed, finally tearing her gaze away from the sky to look over and smile at Lindie.

"Let's hope we can get a good look at the moon with this," Lindie said, giving her telescope a pat before leaning down toward the eyepiece. She turned a knob on the side of the main tube and then gasped.

"What do you see?" Stella asked.

"The eclipse—it's starting!" Lindie replied while still peering through her telescope. "It almost looks like a tiny bite is being taken out of the moon."

Lindie moved away from the telescope and stared at the sky. "Wow," she said, pointing up as her eyes grew wide. "You don't even need a telescope to see it."

Stella looked up at the sky and could indeed see a shadow beginning to darken one side of the moon so it wasn't quite as full. "Can I try the telescope anyway?" she asked Lindie.

"Oh—yes! Of course."

"Thanks," Stella said, stepping over to peer into the eyepiece. Through it, she could see the surface of the moon in far greater detail, slowly but surely being covered up on one side. Lindie's telescope didn't reveal nearly as much as the ones on Starland, but considering that Lindie had built it all by herself, it was still quite impressive.

As it turned out, the lunar eclipse party wasn't exactly a party in the way Stella would have expected, but it was every bit as fun. Some of the Wishlings had brought food and drinks, which they all passed around to each other as they introduced themselves.

"Do you like ladyfingers?" Lindie asked as she held a bag out for Stella.

"Lady *what?*" Stella gasped. All she could picture in that moment were the limbs of Lady Astrid—or whoever the headmistress at Lindie's school was—and her stomach lurched at the thought of eating a Wishling's fingers.

Lindie shook her head and laughed. "They're cookies—not *actual* fingers!"

"Oh, right. Ha." Stella smiled and took one of the long yellow biscuits—and after she bit into it, she was beyond happy that she had. It was more delicious than any cookie she'd ever tasted on Wishworld, and it practically melted in her mouth. "That's the best cookie I've ever had!"

"Really?" Lindie beamed. "Thank you—I made them in home economics class. Do the girls in your home ec classes do much cooking?"

Stella had never heard about home economics before, so she simply shrugged and shook her head.

"I actually quite enjoy it," Lindie said after finishing off her cookie. "There's a lot of science involved in cooking; I don't think most people realize that, especially anyone who says, a woman's place is in the kitchen, like it's a bad thing."

"That's true." Stella nodded as she thought back to the zoomberry cake Cora had made for her Bright Day during their final year at Starling Academy. She could almost hear Cora saying that she'd gotten the recipe from Stella's mom and tested it in the lab until she got it right—and that Stella would have done the same thing for her, since she loved science so much.

Before the memory could make Stella too misty-eyed, a man who was apparently the eclipse-party organizer began to speak to the crowd, providing details on what caused an eclipse. Essentially, he noted, Wishworld (which he of course referred to as Earth) was casting a shadow because it had directly lined up that moment with the moon and the sun, so it was preventing the sun's light from reaching the moon! Afterward, when he came over to introduce himself to Stella and Lindie, and then saw Lindie's telescope, he became extremely animated.

"How old are you?" the man asked.

"Seventeen," Lindie replied.

"Well, I'll be," he said, shaking his head. "It's not often that I see a young lady taking an interest in science."

Then someone shouted out, "Hey! Look!"

"Yeah!" yelled out another voice. "It's a shooting star!"

Stella looked up and, indeed, saw a bright light streaming through the dark sky. Everyone at the party began to ooh and aah as they noticed the shooting star as well, and several of them wondered what it would be like to see one up close. Stella smiled but kept it to herself. If they only knew how close one was to them at that very moment, right in her purse!

"Make a wish," the speaker called out to the crowd, and almost immediately, Stella saw one Good Wish Orb after another materialize, each glowing with its own unique, vibrant color.

She sighed happily as she watched the orbs take flight, even though she knew she hadn't been responsible for creating them; it was all thanks to the shooting star. But it did remind her that she still needed to focus on Lindie's wish—the one she'd already made that Stella was there to help grant but hadn't quite pinpointed yet.

"That man sure seemed impressed with your telescope," Stella said to Lindie after he walked away. "He almost couldn't believe you really built it yourself."

"Yeah, neither can my parents," Lindie answered. "They weren't exactly thrilled about me coming here tonight."

"Really? Why?" Stella felt her Wish Pendant beginning to get warm beneath her pink sweater and sensed that she was getting closer to the wish that had sent her on this mission.

"My mother wanted me to go dress shopping with

her for a dance I'm supposed to attend with my boyfriend this weekend." Lindie made a sour face and rolled her eyes.

"Why did you come here instead?" Stella asked as her mind flashed back to a bittersweet memory of going to the New Beginnings Ball with Ozzie, Cora, and Theodore.

"Because . . . just look at this place!" Lindie gazed up at the sky and spun around happily. "All I've ever wanted to do is learn about the planets and the stars."

"They are quite wonderful," Stella agreed.

"Yeah," said Lindie. Then she nodded sadly and frowned as she looked down at the grassy hill. "If only I could be an astronaut one day."

Stella's Wish Pendant grew warmer still. "Why can't you?" she asked. "What's stopping you?"

"My parents, mostly." Lindie sighed and sat down on the fuzzy blue-striped blanket she had spread out on the grass, motioning for Stella to join her. "I was actually going to apply for an ASAA scholarship—but they told me I shouldn't bother."

In case Stella didn't know, Lindie explained, the ASAA stood for the American Space and Aeronautics Academy, which was a special school that focused on space exploration.

"Why would your parents say something so discouraging?" Stella wondered while shaking her head.

"They think it's crazy for a girl to want to be an astronaut," Lindie explained, "and I guess maybe they're right; it's not like there are any women in the space program. They don't want me to get my hopes up. But I still wish I could somehow find a way to get that scholarship."

Stella noticed that her Wish Pendant was glowing so brightly that it became almost unbearably hot. Despite the discomfort, this was the best possible indicator of what the Wisher was seeking. This was Lindie's wish—to get that scholarship—and it was up to Stella to help her.

"Well, you can't get it if you don't apply," Stella pointed out.

"I know, but the application has to be postmarked by Monday," Lindie said with a sigh, seemingly resigned to her fate. "So I would have to finish it this weekend."

Stella realized she'd have to act quickly. "Well, how much have you already done?"

Lindie's eyes sparkled in the moonlight as soon as Stella asked that. "Do you know anything about artificial satellites?"

"Of course," responded Stella, who then nodded, recalling the information Starland had acquired about the devices Wishlings had been launching into orbit recently. "Like the Sputnik and the Explorer, right? You can send them out into space and use them to record information about all sorts of things."

"Exactly!" Lindie seemed both thrilled and surprised that Stella knew so much. "I built one and actually managed to gather a whole lot of data with it. It's not exactly as advanced as the others you mentioned—obviously— but I've made quite a few interesting discoveries with it."

"That sounds star—er, fantastic!" Stella was truly impressed.

"Thanks." Lindie smiled, perking up slightly. "I have a replica of it at home—you know, in case I decide to submit it with my scholarship application."

"You do?"

"Yeah—would you like to see it?" Lindie asked.

"I'd love to!" Stella replied.

"Okay," Lindie said. "But do you need to let your parents know where you'll be?"

"No. I told them I'd be out most of the night for the eclipse party," Stella explained quickly.

"And they *let* you?" Lindie's mouth dropped open.

"Yes, they know how much I love the stars—and the moon," Stella said with a grin.

"You're so lucky."

Once Stella had helped Lindie gather up her telescope and blanket, they began the short walk from the observatory to Lindie's house. On the way, Stella thought about the fact that there were so few girls at the observatory that night—and that apparently not many seemed to be interested in science, as the man at the party had mentioned. If Lindie applied for and got the ASAA scholarship, there was no telling how many Wishling girls might be motivated to do similar things! Stella felt a rush of excitement as she remembered what Skylar had said: "This is bound to be your most important—but also most challenging—mission yet." It was certainly looking that way.

15

As they walked along Lindie's street, Stella noticed that all the houses and their yards looked quite similar, with flat roofs, large windows, and neatly manicured lawns. Stella was having mixed feelings: as excited as she was about the importance of the mission, she couldn't stop thinking about the potential challenges it presented as well. What if Lindie remained convinced that it wasn't worth applying for the scholarship? What if she decided that she really should listen to her parents and not get her hopes up?

Stella shook her head in an effort to banish her concerns. She couldn't allow such thoughts to interfere with the task at hand. She needed to stay positive!

"Edward, is that you?" a woman called out after Lindie opened the front door and she and Stella made their way into a room decorated with a shaggy white carpet and furniture with colors that were almost as bright as those on Starland: an orange couch, yellow chairs, and pale blue tables.

Before Lindie could reply, a woman came in through an open doorway. She was flawlessly styled in a green knee-length dress and matching high-heeled shoes, along with a pearl necklace and earrings and bright pink lipstick. Her chin-length hair, which was the same light brown as Lindie's, cascaded in a neat wave around her face and was flipped up at the ends. She looked like she was ready to go out to a fancy party.

"Oh, Lindie—it's you." The woman smiled but then narrowed her eyes at Stella. "I didn't know you were bringing a friend home."

"Yes, Mother, this is Stella," Lindie replied. "We met at the lunar eclipse party."

"I see. Hello, Stella. You may call me Carol." Lindie's mother got a slightly uncomfortable look on her face. "So you find these, ah, moon-gazing parties to be enjoyable, too?"

Stella felt awkward—especially at the thought of calling a parent by her first name—but forced a smile nonetheless. "Yes . . . Carol . . . I do," she said with a quick nod. "And it was so fun being able to look through the telescope that Lindie built."

"Was it?" Lindie's mother grimaced. "So that box of bolts actually worked?"

"It sure did—even better than I expected!" Lindie said proudly as she set down the equipment on the nearest table and motioned for Stella to place the blanket next to it.

"Oh, Lindie, please take those things up to your room," her mother said sternly. "I don't want there to be a lot of clutter in the house when your father gets home from his meeting!"

"Sorry, Mother." Lindie sucked in her breath and grabbed the box, then asked Stella to take the blanket and follow her upstairs—which Stella gladly did. Lindie's mother seemed so strict and critical, and Stella felt almost physically weak in the presence of so much negative energy.

Lindie led Stella to the end of a hallway and into her bedroom. It was quite large and reminded Stella a bit of her side of the dorm room at Starling Academy, especially the pink comforter, shiny pink pillows, and gold cushions on the bed. The far wall was entirely glass—a big floor-to-ceiling window with a sliding glass door that led out to a deck—and there a white telescope was set up on a tripod over in the corner. Stella could easily picture Lindie taking it out onto the deck to look up at the sky at night.

"Your room is so nice," Stella remarked.

"Thank you," said Lindie as she set the box containing her telescope equipment down in a corner and walked over to her desk. She opened the bottom drawer and took out a silver winged object.

"Is that the satellite?" Stella asked, dropping the blanket she was carrying next to Lindie's telescope equipment before rushing over to take a look.

"Yes," Lindie said with a smile, handing it to Stella. Then she opened another desk drawer and pulled out an orange folder containing a thick stack of papers. "And here's research. It has all the details about the components of the satellite and what they do, and then a whole section with the data I gathered."

Stella's eyes widened as she examined the different parts of the satellite before handing it back to Lindie and looking through the pages in the folder. A diagram explained each of the components: batteries and solar panels for power, different sensors, recording chips and antennae for receiving and transmitting information, a fuel tank used for launching it, and so much more. Then there were the findings, which included measures of rainfall, changes in atmospheric temperatures, and even the amount of energy Wishworld was absorbing from the sun—which appeared to be similar to the calculations

189

wish scientists made on Starland, measuring the wish energy being received from Wishworld.

As she read through it all, Stella couldn't help thinking back to her Wish-Science Fair project and how desperately she had wanted to go work in the Wish-Tank—not to mention how lucky she was that so many people, including her parents, had believed in her rather than telling her she shouldn't try because she was a girl. She knew that Lindie felt the same way about getting her dream job, and that she had to help her.

"So . . . what do you think?" Lindie finally asked.

"I think you *have* to apply for that scholarship," Stella replied. "You simply must!"

But before Lindie could say anything, her mother appeared in the doorway with a large white box.

"Oh, dear," she said as she walked into the room and set the box down on Lindie's bed. "Is that the little project you've been working on?"

"Yes, I wanted to show it to Stella," Lindie replied with a confident smile.

"Well, put it away, because I have something far more exciting to show *you*!" Lindie's mother lifted the lid from the box and took out a dress.

Stella couldn't help gasping when she saw how beautiful the garment was, with its sparkly gold bodice and full pink skirt. "Oh, it's beautiful," Stella murmured without quite realizing she'd spoken the words out loud.

"Isn't it just?" said Lindie's mother as she beamed proudly and widened her blue eyes at her daughter.

"Wow—it really is!" answered Lindie, hurrying over to pick up the dress before heading over to stand at a gold-framed full-length mirror in the corner. She held the dress up so it mostly concealed the yellow argyle sweater and pink pants she was wearing, and smiled happily at her reflection.

"Let's take out those pigtails," her mother said, removing the pink ribbons from Lindie's hair and gently smoothing it down. "Oh, Lindie, Roger is going to be over the moon when he sees you in that tomorrow night!"

Lindie closed her eyes and tilted her head back as she twirled around the room with the dress. "He is, isn't he?" She grinned as she opened her eyes and stared at her reflection again.

Stella's heart immediately sank. She'd almost forgotten that Lindie's parents thought it was more important for her to go to the dance than work on her scholarship application that weekend. Stella had to do something to steer Lindie away from the dance. But how could she possibly succeed when it appeared that the dress and her parents' influence were pulling her in that very direction?

"But what about finishing your scholarship application?" Stella finally blurted out, unable to come up with something more subtle.

"Don't be silly!" Lindie's mother scowled at Stella. "Lindie knows that spending time with Roger at the dance is going to be the best way to secure her future."

Stella glanced over at Lindie, who had spread the dress out on her bed and was gazing down at it like it had some sort of hypnotic power. "Mother's right," she sighed. "Finishing the application would take me all weekend, and there's no guarantee that I would even get the scholarship."

"But you *will* get Roger's heart when he sees you in that dress!" Lindie's mother added with a satisfied nod. "Now, your father will be home any minute and I need to finish getting dinner ready. Will you be joining us, Stella?"

Of course Stella wanted to stay—she *needed* to stay—but panic, not to mention the negative energy coming from Lindie's mom, seemingly constricted her.

"Oh, yes—please stay for dinner." Lindie nodded hopefully on Stella's behalf.

Stella swallowed hard and finally found her voice. "That would be wonderful, thank you."

As they made their way downstairs, Stella tried to think of a solution to the predicament Lindie faced. But it wasn't until Lindie's father arrived—and commented on how delicious dinner smelled—that it came to her. Of course! Stella would use her mind control powers over Wishling adults to make sure that Lindie's parents encouraged her to work on her scholarship application instead of pressuring her to attend the dance. It was the only way. But she had to choose her moment, and her words, carefully.

After they had all settled around the dinner table, Stella took a deep breath and stared directly into Lindie's dad's dark eyes. Though fixated on her mission, Stella still couldn't help noticing that he looked as dressed up, in a crisp white button-down shirt with a striped blue tie, as Lindie's mother.

"Say, are you baking a chocolate cake for dessert?" Lindie's father suddenly asked his wife, running a hand over his slick black hair as he closed his eyes for a moment and sniffed the air. One of the special powers that young Wish-Granters had over adult Wishlings was mind control, and making them smell their favorite childhood dessert was part of the fun. It also happened to make the adult Wishlings feel happy and more open to suggestion.

Before Lindie's mother could reply, Stella stared into her eyes.

"Why, no, but—Lindie, did you put something in

the oven?" asked Lindie's mother as she turned to look at her daughter. "It does smell delicious!"

"No, I haven't been home all evening—how would I have had time to bake a cake?" Lindie replied, wrinkling up her nose as she glanced from one parent to the other.

"*Hmmm*." Lindie's parents both shrugged. "That's odd."

Stella quickly seized the moment. "You know, you both must agree that Lindie should finish working on her application for the ASAA scholarship this weekend instead of going to the dance."

Almost instantly, Lindie's parents both nodded, their eyes glazing over as their minds became Stella's temporary hostages.

"You know," Lindie's father said, "Lindie *should* finish working on her application for the ASAA scholarship this weekend."

"But, Father—" Lindie nearly choked on the water she had just sipped.

"Yes," her mother interjected. "Lindie should finish working on her application for the ASAA scholarship this weekend, instead of going to the dance."

"What? Mother? Are you feeling all right?" Lindie leaned across the table and narrowed her eyes, studying her mother's face, and then glanced over at Stella to see if she was equally confused. "What about the dress? What about Roger?"

But Lindie's parents simply turned to look at Stella and smiled as they repeated the same words, this time in almost perfect unison and with the same expression. "Lindie should finish working on her application for the ASAA scholarship this weekend, instead of going to the dance."

"I completely agree!" Stella nodded and smiled innocently as she met Lindie's quizzical stare. "Maybe your parents weren't thinking clearly about it until now."

Lindie shook her head, dumbfounded. "Maybe."

Then Stella stared into the eyes of Lindie's mother again and decided to try out a new strategy she'd been working on in the Wish-Tank, silently channeling an additional thought to her.

"You can wear the dress when we take you out for a celebration dinner, after you get the scholarship," Lindie's mother added slowly, perfectly repeating the words that Stella had planted in her mind. "We can invite Roger to that instead."

"Um." Lindie stared down at her plate of food, shocked but happy. "Okay."

Although Lindie seemed thrown by the entire situation that moment, Stella felt certain things were going to fall into place from there. So she smiled quietly to herself as she began eating the casserole that Lindie's mother had served. It had been a challenging mission so far, to be sure, but it seemed the biggest obstacles were finally behind her.

Although Stella had successfully completed the first part of her mission—with Lindie working on the ASAA scholarship application all weekend so she could send it in by the deadline—it was still another few weeks until Lindie's graduation ceremony. That was when the name of the scholarship recipient would be revealed.

When the day finally arrived, Stella sat high up in the back row of the bleachers that looked out on Lindie's high school football field, where chairs and a stage were set up for the graduation ceremony. It felt a lot like the day Stella had graduated from Starling Academy two years earlier—right down to the gut-wrenching nerves she was feeling.

Stella tried to quash her fears by focusing on Lindie, who was sitting up on a special part of the stage, alongside the rest of the honors students—or "high illumination" students, as they were called on Starland. All of them wore shiny gold sashes to indicate that they were the top students in the class. There were enough honors students to make up two full rows, and several of the boys in the group, according to Lindie, had also applied for the ASAA scholarship.

Once everyone was settled in, the principal stepped up to the podium and began to speak to the crowd. Stella's nervousness intensified. There was so much riding on Lindie's wish, and the last thing Stella wanted was to return to Starland without accomplishing her mission. After making a long series of announcements about the accomplishments of the graduating class, which only served to make Stella more worried than ever, the principal finally got to the part of the day Stella and Lindie had been waiting for.

"As we all know, the work being done by the American Space and Aeronautics Academy has become more important than ever before," the principal said as the afternoon sun's rays bounced off his little round glasses. "And they had to be incredibly careful in selecting their recipients for this year's honor. Therefore, I do not want to see any disappointment among the very worthy candidates here. Only one student from our school could be accepted, and I have no doubt that it was a most difficult decision."

Stella sucked in her breath and squeezed her eyes shut, silently channeling every bit of positive energy toward Lindie and the envelope in the principal's hand—not that she had the power to affect what was inside. If only! The principal paused dramatically, and Stella opened her eyes to see most of the people up onstage nodding, smiling, and looking directly at a boy named Charlie, who Lindie had told her was considered the "class brain."

Stella glanced over at Lindie and noticed that she was staring down at the stage, already looking crushed—as if the award had already been given to Charlie. Worry began to consume Stella completely, and she was finding it impossible to concentrate or to make out a word the principal was saying. She pressed her lips together, tears beginning to well up in her eyes as she looked at Lindie. But then the principal's words rang out loud and clear: "It is my distinct honor to announce this huge step for ASAA, and giant leap for women everywhere, as this is the first time this scholarship has been awarded to a female student," he said, turning to look directly at Lindie. "And so it is with tremendous pride that I congratulate our very own Lindie Rand!"

As everyone in attendance leapt to their feet and began to cheer, Lindie stood up and joined the principal at the podium. Stella was clapping so hard that her hands hurt. Lindie had done it! Stella had done it! Lindie's wish had come true! The moment that Lindie began shaking the principal's hand and accepted the paper he was handing her, a massive stream of positive wish energy in bright rainbow hues flowed from her all the way to the back of the bleachers and into Stella's Wish Pendant.

"Wow," Stella heard someone say behind her. "I didn't even know girls were allowed to attend ASAA!" And then more murmurs from people around her: "Well, that's impressive for a young lady." "I guess there's a first time for everything."

That was when Stella noticed something even more magical than anything she had seen on Wishworld ever before—fifty, seventy-five, possibly more than a hundred Wish Orbs shooting above the graduating class, headed straight for Starland. Then, even more Wish Orbs began to rise up above the crowd of friends, family, and especially the young Wishling girls who were there to watch their older family members graduate. Stella couldn't believe what she was seeing. It was just as Skylar had said—and she understood why, without a doubt, this was her most important Wish Mission yet.

16

Upon her return from her mission, Stella couldn't hide her elation—and Skylar was equally thrilled when she welcomed Stella back, her eyes sparkling with warmth and pride as she embraced her on the shimmering blue deck of the Wishworld Launchpad. However, over the next several days, things turned more serious. Stella was called into one meeting after another as she and Skylar determined exactly how events during Stella's Wish Mission impacted the work of the Wish-Tank.

Finally, after tirelessly analyzing the findings, it was time for Stella to share with the rest of the team what they had learned. When she opened the door to the conference room, she was exuberant—and she soon discovered she wasn't the only one. The entire room was buzzing with positive energy as she set down her holo-notebook and took her seat at the large table.

As everyone settled in, Skylar gave Stella a quiet, encouraging smile before turning her attention to the rest of the Wish-Tank staff. "As you all know, Stella's recent Wish Mission was extremely successful," she began. "Never in all my years as a wish scientist have I seen so many new wishes generated in such a short period of time. But the implications of this Wish Mission go far deeper than that—and I would like Stella to come up here and share them with all of us."

Skylar turned and nodded at Stella, who rose to her feet and made her way to the presentation screen while Skylar took her seat at the head of the table.

"Thank you, Skylar." Stella felt her face glowing with pride as she took a deep breath and began her presentation. "I feel like we've all done a wonderful job with the Wish Motivation Protocol that was put in place a while ago—but although we have consistently proven the importance of interacting with as many Wishlings as possible so as to motivate additional wishes, my recent mission has opened our eyes to an entirely new category of Wish Orbs."

As Stella and Skylar had anticipated, this news was both fascinating and a bit unsettling for the Wish-Tank staff members, who immediately began chattering among themselves before launching into a series of questions for Stella.

"How can we tell these new Wish Orbs from any other Good Wish Orbs?" asked Lena. "Do they have any physical properties that distinguish them in some way?"

"Fortunately, yes." Stella nodded and took a small glass scepter from the pocket of her silver lab coat. She waved the rod at the presentation screen, prompting a glowing image of a Wish Orb to appear. Like the one Skylar had presented to her on her recent mission, its surface swirled in brilliant hues of green, blue, and silver. "As you can see, these orbs shine more brightly than most and look almost like small replicas of Wishworld itself."

Stella lightly tapped the hologram, sending the image of the Wish Orb over to Lena so she could examine it more closely. Her lavender eyes widened in curiosity as she inspected the image and then passed it around the table to the others. When the image arrived in front of each staff member, they all responded with equal amounts of surprise and awe.

"So what do we call this new category of Wish Orbs?" asked a blue-haired coworker when the image floated over to him. He moved his hands around it, causing it to spin so he could get a look at it from every possible angle.

"Skylar and I discussed this at length, and although

we're awaiting approval from the members of the Starland Wish Science Senate, we have proposed that they be called Inspirational Wish Orbs," Stella revealed. "We have also recommended that these orbs be kept in a new, highly specialized section of Starland's Wish-House. These wishes are very special—they are wishes for things that haven't been achieved before, like when my Wisher Lindie was chosen to be the first girl ever to get a scholarship to a prestigious space program. When wishes like these are granted, they show people what is possible."

As her colleagues processed this information, several of them seemed somewhat confused; then Norma, the youngest and newest staff member, raised her hand.

"Yes?" Stella nodded at Norma.

"Are these wishes similar to Impossible Wish Orbs?" Norma asked in her soft, ethereal voice as she blinked her large greenish-blue eyes. It was an important question, and one that Stella and Skylar had also grappled with for quite a while.

"In some ways, yes," Stella acknowledged. "On my recent mission, I learned that these wishes are especially challenging—often because they focus on things that Wishlings have been told they shouldn't even bother attempting."

Lena motioned to Norma, asking for her to pass

the hologram of the orb back across the table. When it floated over to her, Lena stared at it intently, examining it for several starminutes. "So they're *almost* like Inmpossible Wish Orbs—which must be kept safe in case the Wisher changes it to something that can be fulfilled—but we must work harder than usual to help them come true?"

"Correct," Stella replied. "The important distinction is that these wishes really *are* possible if they're made by Wishlings who are strong and determined enough to pursue them in spite of seemingly insurmountable odds."

Norma raised her hand again. "But it's up to us to make sure a Wisher doesn't lose sight of the power she has to make those wishes come true?"

"Exactly!" Stella smiled and waved her scepter in Lena's direction, retrieving the image of the Inspirational Wish Orb. She gave it a light tap, which caused it to begin multiplying into smaller orbs—each of which began to grow and then sparkle. "The very best part is that when these wishes come true, they have a ripple effect."

"Yes!" Lena said excitedly. "That's what happened when we observed Lindie getting her scholarship on your Wish Mission! When her name was called, almost a hundred girls in the audience were so inspired by her that they sent wishes out into the universe right there and then. There were so many Wish Orbs produced we couldn't possibly count them all."

"Ah, but we *were* able to count them," Skylar interjected.

"We were?" Stella asked, surprised that her mentor hadn't shared this information with her during their meetings.

"Indeed." Skylar nodded. "I received the data from the Starland Wish-House just before our meeting began today."

Stella searched Skylar's face for some indication of what the number might be—but her expression was uncharacteristically blank, and suddenly Stella worried that perhaps the numbers weren't as impressive as she had previously thought. But then, at last, Skylar's eyes sparkled and her rosy lips broke into a wide smile. "Two hundred and forty-seven," Skylar revealed. "And of those, nearly one hundred appear to be Inspirational Wish Orbs!"

Two hundred and forty-seven Wish Orbs produced—and nearly one hundred of them Inspirational Wish Orbs? It was more than Stella could have possibly hoped for! She knew that the more wishes that made their way to Starland, the more positive energy that could be collected. Inspirational Wishes were exponential; they might mean an end to energy shortages forever! As she made her way back to her seat, the entire conference room erupted with conversations about all that had been accomplished—and all the possibilities to come.

"I hope that you're ready," Skylar added, looking around the table at each member of the Wish-Tank staff. "Because you will all be called upon for an Inspirational Wish Mission very soon."

Once again, the room buzzed with positive energy, and Stella felt herself tingling all over. She could only hope that her next Inspirational Wish Mission would be as exhilarating and successful as her first—and that she would get a chance to find out soon.

17

It had been several months, and although Stella had gone on a record number of Wish Missions by Wish-Tank standards, she still hadn't been on another *Inspirational* Wish Mission. So when she was summoned to the Wishworld Launchpad, she tried not to get her hopes up too high. But then, there she was—and there *it* was: Skylar was waiting for Stella with what she immediately recognized as an Inspirational Wish Orb, and it was even more dazzling than Stella remembered her previous one to be.

"Finally!" Stella blurted out, unable to contain her exuberance.

"Yes," Skylar replied with her usual warm smile. "Finally."

"Do you know anything about the wish?" Stella

asked as she eagerly took the orb and gazed at the shimmering hues of green, silver, and blue.

"Only that you are uniquely equipped with the ability to help make it come true—and that it has the potential to set a new standard for Wish-Granters and wish scientists everywhere," Skylar said. "I'm not sure I can even quantify how significant it might be for the Wish-Tank, nor for Starland as a whole."

Stella looked into Skylar's eyes and noticed the slightest hint of concern flash across them.

"Don't worry," Stella said as a sense of calm washed over her. "I'm ready."

"I'm glad." Skylar blinked gratefully at Stella and led her over to the two Star Wranglers who were holding Stella's shooting star steady for her.

Within moments, Stella was fastened to the star and ready to take flight.

"Good luck!" she heard Skylar call out, but she didn't have time to reply as she sped off through the atmosphere at a velocity that made it too difficult to speak.

From there, everything seemed to happen more quickly than usual. Stella found herself approaching Wishworld and swiftly changed from her silver lab coat into a pair of soft, stretchy pink pants and a matching jacket with a white zipper along with white sneakers. Then, holding tightly to her Wish Pendant and saying the words that would transform her appearance, she focused on changing her golden-pink ponytail to light brown and removing all the sparkle and shine from her skin. When her Star-Zap told her to prepare for landing, she noticed that she was approaching a giant sports arena that was full of thousands of people. For a fleeting moment, she worried that someone might see her. But fortunately, she touched down in an empty area near a short tunnel that appeared to lead directly to the playing field itself.

After picking up the star that had transported her, folding it up, and placing it in a small shoulder bag along with her safety glasses, Stella looked down at her Star-Zap and told it to take her to her Wisher. Following its directions, she walked through the tunnel and arrived at a long chain-link fence. Inside the fence was a dirt running track, which was divided up by white lines into several individual lanes that circled around the grassy athletic field. As Stella peered through the fence, she heard the crowds of people up in the stands whistling and cheering. It was clear that this was some sort of athletic competition—but Stella had never seen such an enormous stadium before. It was at least five times the size of the playing field outside of the Radiant Recreation Center at Starling Academy.

As she looked out on the track, Stella finally saw why

the crowd had been cheering: six girls were walking out and taking their positions in front of large signs that were numbered one through six. All of the girls wore white shorts, some with stripes down the sides, and sleeveless shirts in different colors. In the middle of each of their shirts, front and back, was a large white patch with a black number on it. As they took their positions, a man's voice boomed out through a loudspeaker, introducing the girls by name and revealing a few details about each of them, such as where they were from and what had led to them competing in the race that was about to begin. Then each girl bent over, placed her hands on the dirt track, and squatted down as a hush fell over the entire arena.

Suddenly, a loud bang pierced the air and the girls took off like shooting stars, running faster, faster, and faster still. As they sped around the track, the girl in the inner lane was in the lead, but then the one on the outside raced ahead of her. A few moments later, however, it was the third one from the inside of the track edging into first place. It was stimulating to watch, and Stella couldn't resist cheering right along with all the people up in the stands, many of whom had now leapt to their feet. At last, each girl crossed what appeared to be the finish line, one after the other, and the stadium erupted with thunderous applause.

Realizing she still needed to find her Wisher, Stella looked down at her Star-Zap again and followed its directions up the wooden steps leading to the endless rows of blue seats and over to an empty spot near the front. She could feel her Wish Pendant growing warm beneath her jacket as she sat down next to a dark-skinned woman with short black hair who looked over at Stella with a sweet smile. Could this be her Wisher?

"Our baby's up next," the woman said to Stella, who smiled back in spite of being somewhat confused.

Stella simply nodded politely and looked out at the track, wondering who the woman's "baby" was—and, more to the point, if baby Wishlings were really allowed to compete in an event this big. If they were, why would this woman be up in the stands instead of taking care of her baby? Just then, six more girls walked out onto the track and the woman next to her immediately jumped to her feet.

"You've got this, Tina!" the woman shouted, waving her arms frantically, to one of the girls.

"Come on, baby girl!" added the man two seats down from Stella, also rising to his feet. He had gray hair peeking out from a fancy dark blue hat, along with a matching blue suit.

Stella watched as a girl in a red shirt and white shorts, who looked like a younger version of the woman next to her, smiled and waved back before taking her spot in the outside lane. So *that* was their baby—although a bit more grown-up than Stella had expected. She must have been at least sixteen. As the couple next to Stella sat back down, the booming voice of the announcer echoed through the stadium once again, introducing each of the competitors out on the track. When he began talking about Tina, Stella glanced over at the couple again and saw them nodding along and beaming with pride.

"When Tina was a little girl," the announcer was saying, "every doctor she met told her parents that she would never be able to walk—but that didn't stop her. She wouldn't let *anything* stop her—and now, here she is, participating in the Summer Games!"

Stella looked down at the track again. How was it possible that Tina was about to run a race after being told as a child that she wouldn't even be able to *walk*?

"Are you Tina's parents?" Stella asked the woman sitting next to her.

"We sure are," the woman replied with a nod as she gave the man's knee a light pat.

"So is that true—what the announcer said about doctors telling you Tina would never walk?"

"It sure is." Tina's mother smiled with a faraway look in her eyes.

"But—why would they tell you something like that?"

Stella pressed, eager to learn more about Tina, but also wanting to figure out if Tina's mother was her Wisher. Her Wish Pendant wasn't providing any help.

"It was the disease," the woman replied softly. "It affected all the muscles in her body—especially her legs."

"But she wouldn't let that get in her way," Tina's father added, his dark eyes shining as he smiled over at Stella. "She spent months and months at the hospital, in physical therapy. And then she started working with the coaches!"

"Once she started running, she never stopped." Tina's mother beamed. "For as long as we can remember, she's only wished for one thing—to win a gold medal in the Olympics."

When Stella heard those last few words, she felt her Wish Pendant growing warm beneath her pink jacket. She shifted away from the woman for a moment so that she could check it—and, indeed, it was glowing bright pink. Tina *must* be her Wisher—and her wish was to win a gold medal. But . . .

"Here we go!" Tina's father let out a whistle, interrupting Stella's thoughts, and began to tap his foot as he stared intently down at the track.

Stella turned her attention to Tina, too, watching as she and the other girls all bent over and placed their hands on the dirt track. Then, just as before, a shot rang

213

GOOD WISH
GONE BAD

out and they all took off. Almost immediately, Tina was in the lead! Stella leapt to her feet and began cheering and whistling right alongside Tina's parents—and before she knew it, Tina was nearing the finish line in first. But then, suddenly, the girl in the outside lane overtook Tina by a few strides. Then the girl next to the lead runner edged ahead of Tina as well.

No! Stella focused all of her energy on Tina, hoping against hope that she could somehow push her back into the lead. But it was no use. The other two girls crossed the finish line and Tina came in a very close third. Stella collapsed in her seat. How could this be? She was supposed to be there to make sure that Tina won a gold medal . . . wasn't she? How was she going to do that now that the race was over?

But then Stella noticed that Tina's parents were embracing happily. As they broke apart, they looked out at the track again and cheered even louder than before when Tina walked by and waved up at them with a huge smile. Clearly they didn't mind in the least that Tina had only come in third place, and Stella couldn't help smiling at how proud they all were.

"Can you believe it?" Tina's mother flashed a huge smile as she turned to Stella and squeezed her arm. "My baby got the bronze medal! The *bronze medal!*"

"That's wonderful!" Stella replied. "Congratulations!"

"Thank you," the woman said, dabbing at her tears of joy with a white handkerchief as the man looked over and nodded his pleasure as well, his brown eyes also glistening with happy tears.

Still, Stella couldn't help worrying that she had failed to fulfill her Wish Mission. Had she arrived too late—or was she wrong about the wish? She watched as Tina headed up to a small stage out on the field, where the medals were being given to each of the girls who had placed as one of the top three finishers in each of the last few races.

"Congratulations!" The announcer's voice boomed through the speakers when he got to Tina, and someone else put a medal over her head to hang around her neck. "This is quite a surprise victory for you—and I know that everyone here will be looking forward to seeing you run in tomorrow's race!"

Ah! Stella breathed a sigh of relief as the new information sank in. "There's another race tomorrow?"

"Yes, indeed," Tina's mother replied. "Tina wasn't expected to place in today's race at all, so the bronze is just marvelous—but tomorrow's the big event for her."

"Everyone who's anyone has predicted she'll take the gold tomorrow," Tina's father added with a wink.

So there it was. Stella would somehow need to help make sure Tina got that gold medal at *tomorrow's* race.

She sat back in her seat and felt a warm glow rise to her cheeks as she looked out at all the people in the stadium—especially the little girls, waving flags and cheering for the next group of athletes. In that moment, Stella flashed back to the conversations she'd had with her friends at Starling Academy about Wishling girls and Wishlings with darker skin having fewer opportunities than others. Yet there was Tina, showing the world that she wouldn't be limited by anyone or anything—including a disability. Everything she had already accomplished proved that anybody could make their wishes come true, no matter what body they were born in, so long as they believed in themselves.

No wonder Skylar had emphasized the significance of this mission for the Wish-Tank and all of Starland. It actually didn't even sound like Tina would need Stella's help making her wish come true! But as she looked up at the sky and noticed a bank of dark clouds beginning to roll in, Stella couldn't help remembering that there were no guarantees—especially when it came to Inspirational Wish Orbs.

18

The next afternoon, Stella sat on a bench near a practice area not far from the stadium, watching Tina and a few other athletes warming up for their events. As the hot sun beat down, Tina stepped away from the dirt track and grabbed a small towel from the bench to blot her forehead. She glanced over at Stella and gave her a quick smile as a little girl with light brown skin and a pale green dress began to approach, clutching a small notebook and a pen. But before the girl reached Tina, she turned and raced back to a woman who must have been her mother, burying her face in the woman's floral skirt. The woman laughed softly and shrugged at Tina, who slowly approached the girl—who was still hiding her face—and gave her a gentle tap on her shoulder.

"What's your name?" Tina asked.

The girl turned around and blinked up at Tina. "I'm Ruby," she said softly.

"Well, hello, Ruby. I'm Tina." She smiled down at the girl. "Are you going to watch the Olympics later today?"

"Yes!" Ruby's face suddenly brightened and she didn't seem nervous anymore. "I can't wait to see your race! You're going to win the gold medal! I want to be in the Olympics one day, too!"

Tina nodded and laughed kindly. "I'm sure you will, Ruby. I'm sure you will."

"May I have your autograph?" Ruby asked, holding out her notebook and pen.

"Of course." Tina took the notebook and wrote something in it before handing it back. "There you are, Ruby. I'll see you at the race later today, okay?"

"Okay!" Ruby twirled around and turned back to her mother, who gave her a hug.

Stella smiled as she watched the girl and her mother walk away while Tina headed back onto the practice track. After a light jog in place, she headed over to a woman who Stella figured was Tina's coach. The woman wore a red jacket and blue pants, and had a whistle hanging around her neck. After Tina squatted down and placed her hands on the dirt track, the woman blew the whistle and Tina took off, sprinting so quickly that she almost became a blur. After crossing the finish line, she wound back around toward her coach.

"That was your best time yet!" the woman said, looking down at a round silver object in her hand.

"Really?" Tina was breathing hard as she bent over and put her hands on her knees.

"Incredible," said the coach, who smiled and shook her head as she checked the device again. "But I think that's enough practice. You should really take a break and rest up before the race."

"Okay," Tina replied. "I'm just going to do another run or two with Barbara and then I'll meet you back at the stadium."

"Sounds good," the coach said, waving a quick good-bye as she departed.

After doing several deep stretches, Tina walked over to an athlete who had flushed pink cheeks and curly brown hair. She wore white shorts like Tina's, but her sleeveless shirt was blue instead of red. A young woman with a blond ponytail stood off to the side; Stella figured she must be the other athlete's coach. Tina and the athlete chatted for a few moments, and then they both bent over and placed their hands on the track. The blond woman held up a round device like the one Tina's coach had been holding and blew the whistle that was hanging around her neck. Tina and the other athlete began to run a practice race around the track.

Though it was only a practice run, Stella couldn't help getting caught up in the thrill of competition as she watched Tina bolt into the lead, just like she had during the previous day's race. Tina was at least ten paces ahead of her competitor as they wound around the track and neared the finish line. Stella had to resist the urge to leap up and begin cheering for Tina. But then, as a dark cloud drifted overhead, blocking out the sun and casting a shadow down on the track, Tina suddenly stumbled and went crashing to the ground. The other athlete stopped abruptly and crouched down next to her. Horrified, Stella instinctively jumped to her feet and rushed over to them.

"Are you okay?" Stella asked when she got to Tina, who was writhing in pain and clearly *not* okay.

"I—I don't know," Tina gasped, her legs covered in dirt, as she curled up on the ground. She reached down to touch her ankle, right where a small patch of blood had streamed out and marred her smooth skin. She winced.

"Don't worry—my friend is getting you some ice," the other athlete said, motioning to the blond girl who Stella had mistaken for her coach.

"Thanks, Barbara," Tina replied with a weak smile.

Stella swallowed hard, trying not to panic, and breathed a sigh of relief as Barbara's friend approached with a small white bag and handed it to Tina.

"Thank you," Tina said as she took the bag and tried to sit up, flinching when she placed the ice against her bruised ankle.

"Do you think it's broken?" Barbara's friend asked, her pale blue eyes wide and reflecting concern.

"I'm not sure," Tina replied.

"Are you going to be able to race?" Barbara asked softly.

Tina shook her head and tears began to well up in her eyes. "I hope so—but I don't know," she finally responded after pondering the question.

Stella felt queasy as she looked at Tina. But then she noticed her Wish Pendant was growing warm beneath her pink jacket. She stood up and walked away for a moment so she could consult her Star-Zap, which immediately gave her the guidance she needed.

"We need to get a medic," Stella said to Barbara.

"Right—of course!" Barbara replied. She nodded to her friend and they both raced over to a small brown building halfway between the practice area and the stadium while Stella stayed with Tina.

"I'm Stella, by the way," she said as she sat down on the dirt track by Tina's side.

"Hi, Stella. I'm Tina."

"Yes." Stella couldn't help smiling. "I know. I'm a big fan of yours. I met your parents at the race yesterday."

"That's where I recognize you from," Tina said, her eyes filling with tears as she tried to control her emotions. "I should probably get word over to them and my coach that I can't race today."

"No!" Stella insisted, reaching out to give Tina's shoulder a reassuring squeeze. "You're going to be okay—I'm sure of it."

"I'm glad somebody is," Tina said as she stared down at the track, clearly struggling to remain calm and brave.

"Let's at least wait and see what the medic has to say," Stella told her.

"Okay, I guess you're right," Tina agreed.

Finally, after what felt like an eternity, Barbara and her friend returned with a man dressed in a white jacket and pants. He had a confident look in his dark eyes as he set down a white metal box with a big red cross on it.

"Don't you worry, Tina," the man said after he examined her ankle and carefully began to wrap it with stretchy white material. "It's just a little sprain."

"But—what about the race?" Tina asked as he continued to bandage her up.

"Well . . ." the man began before inhaling and shaking his head, "I don't believe you'll be competing in *today's* race, but you'll definitely be able to run again, eventually."

That wasn't the answer Tina was looking for, and it certainly wasn't what Stella wanted to hear, either. But what could she do? She sat there, at a complete loss, as the medic finished wrapping Tina's ankle and then helped her up and over to the bench. After a while, and with repeated assurances from Tina that he didn't need to hang around any longer, the medic departed and wished Tina good luck. Next Barbara and her friend said their good-byes as well.

"I hope we'll see you at the race later," Barbara added softly, touching Tina's arm before departing.

"Thanks," Tina replied with a weak smile. "But if I don't see you there, good luck."

Barbara frowned and thanked Tina before turning to walk away.

After the others had left, Tina looked at Stella and, once again, insisted that she didn't need to stay.

"Yes I do," Stella replied immediately.

"But I don't think there's anything you or anyone else can do for me right now," Tina said. "I'm going to have to bow out of today's race, like the medic said, and focus on competing again another year."

"Another *year*?" Stella shook her head. "No way. You're supposed to get that gold medal *today*."

"But how?" Tina looked at Stella like she was crazy. "I can't even walk."

When Tina said those words, Stella felt her Wish Pendant growing warm again. And this time she knew exactly what to say. "But you *can* walk—just like you walked all those years ago, even though the doctors said you never would," Stella said firmly. "And you can run—and you will run—no matter what that medic said."

Tina's eyes grew wide and she sat up straighter as she listened to Stella's pep talk. "Oh, my goodness," she finally whispered. "You're right."

Then, almost immediately, a huge smile spread across Tina's face and she rose to her feet. Although she had to lean on Stella as they began to walk toward the stadium, with each step they took, Stella could feel Tina getting stronger. By the time they reached the gates leading into the arena where Tina was supposed to compete, she was walking without any help from Stella at all.

Once they both got inside, Tina began to warm up, lightly jogging in place—with no visible signs of pain. Of course, there was still the matter of running the race and winning the gold medal. But as Stella wrapped a hand around her Wish Pendant and felt its warmth, she focused all of her energy on Tina—and on the Wish Mission succeeding.

Still, when Stella arrived at her seat in the front row

an hour later to watch Tina's upcoming event, it felt as if all the flutterfocuses on Starland had somehow made their way down to Wishworld and moved directly into her stomach. Tina's parents, who were already at their seats, glanced over at Stella. She could see from the looks on their faces that they were feeling a bit unsettled as well.

"Well, hello again," Tina's mother said in a shaky voice while her husband tipped his hat toward Stella.

"Hello again," Stella replied softly, sucking in her breath just as the booming voice of the announcer echoed through the stadium.

Stella looked down at the track and saw Tina walking slowly but confidently next to Barbara and the other four girls they would be competing against. When Tina looked up at the stands, waving at her parents and then locking eyes with Stella and smiling broadly, Stella felt the flutterfocuses begin to settle down in her stomach.

Once again, Tina had defied the medical predictions—she *was* going to compete in the race. Now she just needed to make sure she also won that gold medal.

After the announcer wrapped up the introductions, each competitor crouched down in their starting positions. The moment the now familiar sound of the shot to start the race rang through the stadium, Tina took off and was immediately in the lead. In fact, it was almost exactly like the practice run earlier, with Barbara a distant second and the other four athletes several strides behind her. Stella could feel her Wish Pendant glowing beneath her jacket and had the overwhelming sense that Tina would remain in the lead this time. There was no way that she would stumble or fall. That gold medal was simply too important!

As she rounded the final turn, Tina was still ahead of the others, and it felt like everyone in the stadium was holding their collective breath, waiting and watching as she approached the finish line. Tina's parents leapt to their feet, all set to cheer for their daughter and the gold medal she was about to win. Stella got up, too. But then, almost exactly like Tina's preceding practice run, a cloud passed in front of the sun, casting a shadow down on the track. Tina suddenly stumbled and lost her footing!

Stella's mouth dropped open. No! This couldn't be happening again, could it? Although Tina didn't fall down this time, the stumble cost her and she fell behind. Simultaneously, the dormant swarm of flutterfocuses began raging again in Stella's stomach, but this time like never before. She held her breath as she watched Tina grit her teeth, throw back her head, and clearly work to power through any pain she might be feeling. Sure enough, within moments, she had miraculously regained her composure and edged ahead of Barbara again!

That was it—the lead runners were nearing the finish line, and Tina was heading the pack, so close to garnering the gold medal. She closed in on the finish line and then—yes!—Tina crossed it first, with Barbara right behind her.

"And she's done it!" the announcer bellowed. "Tina Randolph—the girl who doctors said would never walk—has won the gold medal! She's making Olympic history here today, ladies and gentleman. There's no stopping this girl, that's for sure!"

Tina's parents were so excited they began screaming as they embraced each other. Then Tina's mother turned to Stella and hugged her, too, as tears streamed forth. As the applause echoed through the vast stadium, Stella was overcome with emotions. She wanted to laugh, cry, and scream even louder than Tina's parents! But instead, she simply stood there in awe, staring down at Tina as a beautiful stream of wish energy began to flow from her, before cascading through the stadium and up into Stella's Wish Pendant.

Then, as the sun's rays began to burn through the cloud that had cast a shadow on the track moments before, Stella saw hundreds of glowing Wish Orbs flying up into the sky. There were so many of them making their way to Starland that the cloud was completely eclipsed by them—and as Stella glanced around, she noticed one Wish Orb in particular. It was definitely an Inspirational Wish Orb, and it was floating directly above the head of little Ruby, the girl in the green dress who had talked to Tina earlier that day.

The orb that had brought Stella to Wishworld for Tina had been beautiful, but Ruby's was even more dazzling, with a light unlike any other. It positively took Stella's breath away.

19

Stella had expected Skylar to be waiting for her out on the Launchpad when she returned from her mission—but in fact, it appeared that everyone had already left for the day. So after unfastening herself from her star, Stella made her way out into the hallway all alone. It seemed a bit anticlimactic after such an exhilarating mission. But then Stella spotted Skylar suddenly racing up to greet her.

"Welcome back!" Skylar said, her face shining as brightly as her golden hair and lab coat as she approached. And before Stella knew what was happening, she was wrapped up in an enthusiastic embrace.

"Thank you," Stella replied after they parted. She had never seen Skylar quite so excited, or even quite *that* friendly with the rest of the staff. Stella felt both proud and a bit embarrassed by the exuberant reception.

"I'm sorry to have missed you out on the Launchpad—but come with me," Skylar said, squaring her shoulders and becoming slightly more formal. "We have so much to discuss."

Stella nodded dutifully and followed her mentor. But instead of going to Skylar's office or the Wish-Tank conference room, they headed down to the ground floor and out through the sliding glass doors at the back of the building. Then Skylar continued to make her way across the vast sparkling blue deck where employees usually went for their lunch breaks or informal meetings at the silver and gold outdoor tables. But they didn't stop there, either. Instead, they headed all the way down to one of the many grassy hills that surrounded the Wish-Tank headquarters.

Stella breathed in the sweet Starland air and looked out at the reflection of the stars dancing on the placid, shimmering surface of Luminous Lake. Far off in the distance, she could see the outline of some of Starling Academy's tallest buildings, which instantly reminded her of Cora, who had been on Stella's mind quite a lot in recent months. In many ways, Inspirational Wish Missions weren't all that different from the idea Cora had had back at Starling Academy about leading by example to encourage more wishes. Perhaps it was just a coincidence, but a small part of Stella also couldn't shake the feeling that Cora had somehow been with her on her most recent mission.

"So"—Skylar's voice gently guided Stella's focus back to the present—"as you already know, the Inspirational Wish Missions the staff have been going on have all been tremendously successful—and each one has reinforced the profound power these unique wishes possess.

"But your most recent mission has brought more positive wish energy to Starland than we ever could have anticipated," Skylar said. "Far more than your previous one."

Even though Stella had already suspected as much, Skylar's words made her skin tingle with pure joy. "I'm so happy," Stella replied.

"I am, too—but there's more," Skylar said. "As a result of our findings, the members of the Starland Wish Science Senate have approved our proposal for the new Inspirational Wish Orb category—*and* a new section of the Starland Wish-House has indeed been created for them."

"Oh, that's wonderful!" responded Stella, who widened her eyes, awed by everything that had happened in the time she'd been working at the Wish-Tank.

"It truly is—and I must say, I don't think we would have been nearly as successful without all of your contributions," Skylar noted with a warm smile.

Stella didn't want to be too hasty, but she was getting the distinct impression that Skylar was about to present her with something substantial. Perhaps she was going to give her yet another Inspirational Wish Orb already— or maybe a promotion? But as her mentor shifted her eyes up to the sky, they clouded over as she became melancholy and let out an audible sigh.

"What is it?" Stella finally asked, although she wasn't entirely sure that she wanted to know the reason for the sudden shift in Skylar's mood.

"I'm sorry," Skylar said softly, still looking up at the stars. "We have so much to celebrate, and yet I have some difficult news to share with you."

Stella brought a hand to her mouth and braced herself for the worst. Finally, after briefly closing her eyes, Skylar spoke. "While you were on your last Wish Mission, I received word that Lady Astrid had completed her Cycle of Life."

"What? No!" Stella gasped as tears began to well up. In spite of everything that had happened with Cora, the headmistress of Starling Academy had always been incredibly kind and supportive, and Stella considered her to be a powerful influence and guide.

"I know she meant a lot to you, but what you may not realize is how much you meant to her," Skylar continued while taking her Star-Zap from her pocket and handing it to Stella. "Here, you must read this now."

Stella looked down at the Star-Zap as a holo-message appeared before her eyes. It was titled THE LAST WISH AND TESTAMENT OF LADY ASTRID and the words that followed were almost more than Stella could bear: *Of all the Starlings I have had the pleasure of knowing, there is only one who I feel is capable of leading the students of Starling Academy. There is only one who I believe will be able to guide them toward their brightest futures. So, it is my final wish for Stella Albright to take my place as headmistress of Starling Academy.*

As the words sank in, Stella shook her head and swallowed hard. "Me?" she finally asked, looking over at Skylar.

"You," Skylar replied. She gave Stella a gentle nod before shifting her eyes back to the sky. "Look—over there. Do you see her star?"

Stella looked up, searching through the vast array of twinkling lights until she zeroed in on the one that she felt quite certain was Lady Astrid's. It seemed to be smiling down at her—strong, confident, and wise—and it helped Stella smile through her tears.

Of course Stella didn't want to leave the Wish-Tank so soon, but she knew that she had to honor Lady

Astrid's last wish. As she contemplated this next step, she couldn't help thinking about the oracle Lady Astrid once mentioned to her, and she wondered if she had ever discovered the remaining section—if perhaps this, too, had been recorded as part of Stella's destiny. Maybe Lady Astrid had even left clues in her office so that Stella would be able to find the text she had hidden and finally see it for herself!

Stella also thought about how strange it would be to walk the halls of Starling Academy, no longer a student but the head of the entire campus. Once again images of Cora and especially of all the plans they had made together rushed forth. But then, as her thoughts drifted to that awful day when Cora was expelled, she noticed a small cloud floating in front of Lady Astrid's star, obscuring its light. Stella shivered as an icy chill ran down her spine.

Perhaps her most challenging and important missions weren't entirely behind her after all.

PRESENT-DAY STARLAND

"Wow," Vega said as she shut down *The Great Holo-Book of Wish-Granters*. "I already knew that Lady Stella was powerful. But now? I'm in awe."

"I know," Libby agreed, picking up the holo-book and taking it back to the table where she'd found it. "Everything she discovered? All of the things she's done for Starland? It's incredible."

"But what about those clouds—the ones she saw during her last Wish Mission, and then the one floating in front of Lady Astrid's star?" Tessa said, her green eyes now turning dark with worry. "That was obviously some sort of sign—like Cora, or *Rancora*, trying to ruin everything again. Right? Just like Scarlet thought she was doing at Lady Stella's graduation."

"Yes," Cassie agreed, adjusting her star-shaped

glasses. "And I think it was Cora disguised as Barbara's friend who made Tina hurt her ankle, almost like she was granting a bad wish or something. It makes me even more worried about Sage and the others. Do you think they really went to the Negative Energy Facility?"

"I'm sure they did," Tessa replied with a frown. "I hate to say it, but we need to go find them and see if they learned anything else about Rancora. What we discovered here isn't nearly enough."

"But we *did* learn enough about Lady Stella to know that she's got at least as much power as Rancora, maybe even more," Vega pointed out. "And we have a better idea of how we can help her . . . but we also know that the Negative Energy Facility is the last place she would want us to go."

"Well, then what do we do?" Libby asked, tugging on a lock of her pink hair.

Vega narrowed her blue eyes, considering the possibilities. "We need to go to Lady Stella," she concluded. "We need to tell her that we're ready to help—and, unfortunately, we also need to tell her about the others going to the Negative Energy Facility. She's not going to be happy about it, but she needs to know."

"But I don't want to get Sage in trouble!" Cassie insisted. "I don't want to get any of them in trouble."

"They may already *be* in trouble—the kind that only

we and Lady Stella can get them out of," Libby replied. "I think Vega's right. It's our only option."

"I agree," Gemma chimed in.

"Me too," Clover said.

"Then it's settled?" Vega asked, searching the faces of each girl.

At last, each one affirmed they would go find Lady Stella. So they slowly made their way out of the headmistress's office and toward her residence in StarProf Row.

Adora shivered as she and Sage marched ahead of the others on their way to the Negative Energy Facility, with MO-J4 buzzing close by Sage's shoulder. After walking through Dimtown, on the outskirts of Starland City, they could tell they were getting close based on the shriveled gray plants lining the dark and dusty trail. The plants were clearly damaged by the trace amounts of negative energy that seeped out of the facility.

Finally, the girls came to the jagged, sinister-looking cliffs above the NEF. The creepy surroundings were unsettling, but Adora felt certain that they would all be well protected. She glanced back at her companions and smiled proudly at the adorable yellow jumpsuits she had created. The garments would definitely be enough to keep them safe—she was sure of it. Or at least she thought she was.

But when they saw the cave that surrounded the Negative Energy Facility from a distance, all six girls let out a collective gasp. As Vega had predicted, there was a lot more security than what they had seen in the holo-records about the place (back when Cora made that first trip), including an enormous chain-link fence surrounding the cave, which crackled and glowed with the same sort of purple voltage as Bad Wish Orbs did. Further adding to the ominous feel of the place were the two enormous armored Bot-Bot guards patrolling the gated entrance.

"I did not expect to see such large guards," said MO-J4 in his clipped voice as he hovered a bit closer to Sage's shoulder, his little silvery-blue body beginning to shake. "Miss Sage, you know I will do anything for you—but I am not certain that I am equipped for this."

"And I'm sensing something bad is going to happen," Piper whispered. "I don't think we should go any closer."

"What?" Adora hugged her arms across her chest and spun around to glare into Piper's wide aqua eyes. "Don't you remember what you said earlier, about getting the feeling that we *must* come here—*that it will hold all the answers?*"

"Yes, but—" Piper stared down at the ground and shook her head.

"I'm with Piper and MO-J4," Astra interjected, kicking one of her sparkly red star ball shoes into the dusty ground. "I think we should turn back now. This place is seriously creepy."

"It *is* a lot freakier than I expected it to be," Leona agreed, her golden curls trembling along with the rest of her shaking body. "And if MO-J4 can't help us, how are we supposed to get inside?"

"He didn't say he couldn't help us," Sage noted, batting her eyelashes at the Bot-Bot. "Right, MO-J4?"

"Correct," he replied. "I did not say I cannot help you. If you are certain that you require my assistance then I am most happy to do all that I can."

"I'm sure you can do it," Sage insisted. "You're stronger and smarter than any Bot-Bot I've ever met."

"Oh, thank you, Miss Sage!" The screen that functioned as MO-J4's face lit up with a small pink heart. "You are quite wise yourself."

"Okay then, let's go!" Adora said, starting toward the fenced-in cave.

"Uh-uh," Leona replied, shaking her head and turning on the heels of her gold boots. "I'm sorry, but I don't think I can do it—I was more interested in these cute jumpsuits than going inside, anyway. They're totally my color!"

"I can't go, either," Piper said, barely able to meet Adora's angry gaze. "Plus, I feel like someone should stick with Leona."

"Me too—sorry!" Astra frowned before spinning around to catch up with Leona and Piper, who were already heading back the way they came.

Adora stuffed her hands into the pockets of her yellow jumpsuit, pouting as she watched her fellow Star Darlings depart. Then she turned to look at her two remaining companions. "Sage? Scarlet? Am I going to have to do this alone?"

After a short pause, Sage spoke. "No. We have to do this. I'll go with you."

Although Scarlet was feeling uncharacteristically frightened, she also knew this was an opportunity she couldn't possibly run away from. It was dangerous, yes, but that was part of the appeal. "Okay. I'm in, too."

Adora heaved a sigh of relief. "Thank you."

"You're coming, too, right MO-J4?" Sage asked.

"Of course, Miss Sage," their Bot-Bot replied.

So the three girls continued up the path, with MO-J4 buzzing close by, until they all arrived at the front gate. But as she looked up at the giant armored Bot-Bot guards towering above her on either side, Adora didn't feel quite as confident as she had before—especially when the one who was apparently in charge began to speak in a deep, threatening voice.

"Negative Energy personnel only," he said, holding up one of his mechanical arms and fanning out his metal fingers, while his purple Bot-Bot eyes glowed from inside his shiny black helmet. "Please submit your credentials."

The three girls exchanged worried looks, and then Sage said, "We're here on official business—investigating the recent negative energy crisis on behalf of Starling Academy."

"Please submit your credentials," the Bot-Bot Guard repeated.

Sage shot a hopeful look at MO-J4 before looking up at the guard. "Oh—well, our credentials should have been transmitted to your system."

"Yes," MO-J4 chimed in as he touched his arm to a scanner on the side of the Bot-Bot Guard. "Our permission codes have been transmitted. Please check your log."

The guard's glowing purple eyes blinked as he scanned his system for the information. After beeping and buzzing for a few moments, a holographic message appeared on the screen implanted in his armored chest. It read NEGATIVE ENERGY FACILITY ADMISSION GRANTED.

"Yes!" Scarlet cheered under her breath, bending one arm and pumping her fist at her side triumphantly as Sage and Adora both sighed in relief.

"Follow me," said the first Bot-Bot Guard, placing one of his big metal fingers on the gate, which immediately sprung open.

The guard led the group the rest of the way up the dusty path and into the cave, with its jagged blue-gray cliffs. But the moment they got inside and saw the Negative Energy Facility rising up before them, with its gruesome tear-shaped dome glowing in black and purple, the girls all stopped dead in their tracks and literally started shaking in their shoes.

"Oh, my stars," Scarlet whispered first.

Sage nodded, her lavender eyes wide with fear. "It looked scary in the holo-footage, but I didn't realize it would be this—"

"—terrifying!" Adora interjected, finishing Sage's sentence.

Meanwhile, the Bot-Bot guard was already at the heavy black door, punching in the code; within moments it began to slide open.

"Enter," the guard commanded, turning to the girls. But then he extended his mechanical arm to stop MO-J4. "All Bot-Bots must wait outside."

"What? Why?" Sage demanded.

"Bot-Bots cannot sustain power inside, due to the lack of positive energy," the guard explained.

"Oh." Sage puffed out her lower lip in an exaggerated frown as her eyes darted from Vega to Scarlet. MO-J4, however, assured her that they would be fine inside without him.

"You must also wear these," the guard added as three pairs of sparkly silver gloves materialized and floated over to them. "Protective hand-wear."

"How could I have forgotten?" Adora admonished herself, pulling on her gloves and then hoisting her hood over her pale blue hair, before turning to her companions. "I guess this is it, then?"

Sage and Scarlet nodded solemnly after donning their hoods and their gloves. Then they all began to slowly creep toward the doorway, tiptoeing past the guard and into the facility. As they made their way through the gray fog, carefully avoiding the glassy black orbs that were crackling and bobbing all around them with a disturbing purple glow, they grabbed each other's hands, tightening their grip when the sounds of wailing and moaning became louder and louder still. When something suddenly made a loud crunching noise underfoot, they looked down to see the same bits of shiny, jagged black rock that they'd observed in the holo-footage when Cora snuck into the Negative Energy Facility.

Adora, who was between Scarlet and Sage, immediately let go of her friends' hands and bent down to grab one of the rocks. She studied its rough surface, which was slightly lined with threads of sparkly purple, before putting it in the pocket of her jumpsuit and turning to head back toward the door of the Negative Energy Facility. "Well, that was the easiest mission ever," she said.

"Wait!" Scarlet grabbed Adora by the shoulder to stop her. "Shouldn't we look around some more? I mean, can we really be sure that the rock Cora took from here wound up being the source of *all* her power?"

"Hmmm." Adora narrowed her pale blue eyes as she considered Scarlet's words. "Maybe not."

"Hey—look over here!" Sage called out, having been drawn to something glowing toward the back wall of the facility.

"What is it?" Adora shouted back, recoiling when the Bad Wish Orbs wailed a bit louder, as if they were telling her to quiet down—as if *they* were the only ones permitted to make any noise in there.

Adora and Scarlet carefully made their way past the

menacing black spheres and over to where Sage was standing.

"It's some sort of alcove," Sage told them when they arrived.

"Whoa." Scarlet gasped. "It's like an evil lair."

The area resembled what one might imagine the inside of an enormous hollowed-out Bad Wish Orb would look like—as if a giant ball had been pushed against the back of the Negative Energy Facility, carving out a round room that hissed, pulsated, and glowed in swirling, eerie hues of purple, black, and blue. Along one side of the sloped wall was a tall silver cabinet with a long, teardrop-shaped door cut into it; on the opposite side was a glassy black teardrop-shaped bench. Most shocking of all, though, were the dozens upon dozens of little holographic images floating all around the room in teardrop-shaped frames, all of which appeared to be portraits of Wishlings in various stages of agony!

"What do you think this is?" Adora asked, her voice shaking as she stepped inside.

"Clearly, this is Rancora's secret hideout," Sage replied.

Adora went to get a closer look at the holographic images and marveled at how incredibly unhappy they all seemed. "I wonder if these are all Wishers whose bad wishes have come true."

"Maybe—but if their wishes came true, why would they all look like they're in so much pain?" Scarlet wondered, also studying the images.

"Probably because getting a *bad* wish never feels good, even if you think it will," Sage noted as she headed over to the silver cabinet. She touched a little black button on its tear-shaped door, which caused the door to disappear. Sage gasped.

"What is it?" asked Adora, rushing over to the cabinet with Scarlet right behind her.

"Holo-books," Sage said, taking one from the top shelf and wiping a thin film of black dust from its surface so that it glowed a bit more brightly.

"What are they doing in here?" Adora asked, crouching down next to Sage.

"Well . . . this one's called *Negative Energy Manipulation*," Sage said, shuddering as she plucked another holo-book from the shelf. "And this is *My Negatite, My Self.*"

"Oooh!" Scarlet said, captivated by the one she'd found. "This one's called *How Bad Is Your Wish Orb?*"

"Yikes." Adora dreaded what else they might find, but then she noticed a holo-book that appeared to be slightly smaller, newer, and cleaner—as if it had been handled more recently than the others. Her pulse began to race as she carefully removed it from the shelf and realized what she had found. "Oh. My. Stars."

"What?" Sage asked.

"I—I think it's Rancora's journal!" Adora gasped.

"Let's see," Scarlet said, putting the holo-book she was holding back onto the shelf where she'd found it.

All three girls went to sit down on the little glass bench and, trying to steady her trembling hands, Adora accessed the first holo-record . . . and then the next . . . and the next. It indeed appeared to be a detailed account of everything Rancora had ever done, with records dating all the way back to a few months after she—or, rather, *Cora*—had been expelled from Starling Academy.

"She's been sneaking in here!" Sage said, her violet eyes expanding and expressing fear as she looked at the date stamped on one of the first records. "I can't believe she's been coming here for so long—or that she even managed to get in."

"And she's been going down to Wishworld to grant bad wishes," Scarlet added, shaking her head.

"Of course!" Sage said. "Maybe *that's* how she's been collecting negative energy!"

"I bet you're right," Adora noted. "The bad wishes she's been granting go all the way through until just a few years ago."

"Which is when she started working at Starling Academy," Sage interjected. "She probably stopped granting bad wishes after that."

The girls all looked up from the holo-book and searched each other's frightened eyes for some sort of direction.

"What should we do?" Adora finally asked.

"Maybe we should take a look at the last bad Wish Mission she went on," Scarlet proposed.

"Definitely," Sage and Adora both said, nodding solemnly.

Adora tapped on the holo-record of Rancora's final Wish Mission, and they all watched with mouths agape as the details were revealed. . . .

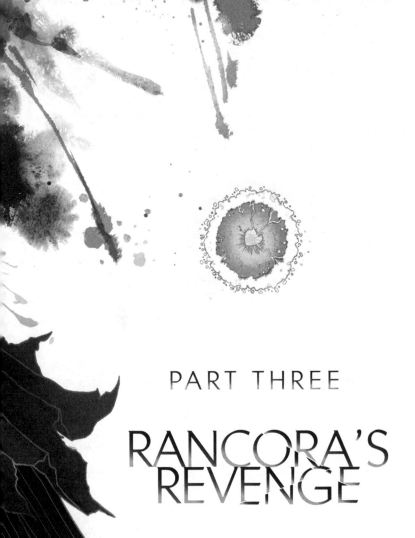

PART THREE

RANCORA'S REVENGE

20

As she made her way along the dusty path leading to the Negative Energy Facility, Rancora felt nothing like the young Starling who had once been terrified to set foot anywhere near the place. In many ways, it had become like a second home to her. When she first left Starling Academy all those years ago, she assumed that the dark feelings in her heart were because her best friend, Stella, had betrayed her and she was so harshly expelled by that dim-witted Lady Astrid. But the truth was, Cora had also been affected by the blast of negative energy she was hit with that day in the Negative Energy Facility, and she knew it.

Initially, she had been startled by the potent energy that seemed to be coming from the mysterious black rock she'd taken during that first fateful visit. The rock seemed to be pulling at her, urging her to somehow harness its power.

That's when she began to do some research and discovered exactly what she had in her possession: unlike Good Wish Orbs, which turn into Wish Blossoms after their wishes come true—with or without the help of a Wish-Granter—Bad Wish Orbs turn into black rocks called negatite after their wishes come true. Rancora learned she was able to grind up her rock into a powerful powder: an evil magic dust.

So now, as she stood on the hill on the outskirts of Dimtown staring at the distant bluish-gray cliffs surrounding the Negative Energy Facility, she took out a bit of negatite powder and gently blew on it. Almost instantly, the powder expanded into a gray cloud that began swirling around her until, all at once, she transformed into a glimmermoth with shiny purple eyes, a furry gray body and antennae, and transparent purple wings. Unlike flutterfocuses, their close relatives, which traveled in swarms, the glimmermoths of Starland were solitary creatures and, best of all, they were known for their ability to slip through the tiniest cracks around windows and doors, allowing them to take up residence in Starlings' homes and closets whether they'd been invited or not. It was how she continued to sneak into the NEF, despite the increased security.

Once she flew past the armored Bot-Bot guards and slithered into the Negative Energy Facility, Rancora easily transformed back into her Starling body—although all traces of the girl formerly known as Cora had vanished. Instead of shimmering blue hair and glittery skin, her eyes were now a terrifying purple and her skin and hair a cold ashen gray, which matched her long ragged gown with its high amethyst collar.

She had become Rancora, and there was no turning back. It was the result of her many years of bad Wish Missions, each one exposing her to increasing amounts of negative energy, which she came to thrive on and gathered in the teardrop-shaped crystal pendant that hung from a black chain around her neck.

Now, walking slowly through the rows of Bad Wish Orbs that were bobbing around her like hissing and crackling minions, Rancora narrowed her eyes at each one, growing more impatient as the moments ticked by. Which orb would select her next, and why was it taking so long? She was so close to reaching her goal—to gather enough negative energy to upset the balance of Starland, thus allowing her to seize control—and she was fed up with all the waiting! She would finally get her revenge on Stella after all these years by ruining the positive energy she had spent her life's work to create.

Finally, the dark crystal teardrop hanging around

her neck began to pulsate and glow, and her attention was drawn to an orb that was vibrating and smoldering in the same ominous way as her pendant. Carefully, she wrapped her bony fingers around the crackling black surface of the orb and almost instantly she knew she would be making the familiar journey to Wishworld.

Thanks to her teardrop pendant, Rancora had no need for a Star-Zap to give her instructions or assistance in altering her appearance; the negative energy provided her with more than enough power for such pursuits. So as she neared the Wishworld atmosphere, she quickly held the pendant, chanting the words, "Star dark, star dim, take this blackened orb so grim; negatite I call on you to help me make this wish come true!" With that, she changed herself into a middle-aged Wishling with ash-blond hair in a messy updo. Her dark gown transformed in a mission-appropriate ensemble: dark skinny jeans, knee-high black boots, and a black T-shirt with a cropped gray leather jacket over it.

Moments later, Rancora found herself touching down in a large parking lot packed with cars from one end to the other. Beyond all the vehicles was a huge collection of buildings with a sign at the top in big red letters that said GLENNCOVE MALL. She wrapped a hand around her crystal pendant so that it could direct her to the Wisher she was there to help and then made her way past the rows of cars and toward the complex's entrance.

The sliding glass doors leading into the mall parted and she walked in, scanning the shoppers who walked by to see if one of them was her Wisher. As she made her way toward a row of kiosks, Rancora heard the sound of excited screams and saw a huge crowd of people rushing toward her, clamoring to get into a clothing store. There was such a massive wave of Wishlings that she felt herself being forced off to one side. But then, as she was regaining her footing, she bumped into a girl with long purple-streaked black hair.

"Excuse me!" Rancora snapped at the girl as she staggered back to her feet.

"No, excuse *me*!" the girl shot back, narrowing her dark eyes at Rancora and scowling as she planted her hands on her hips.

The Wishling couldn't have been more than seventeen years old, but she was still an intimidating figure—tall and stocky with a red denim jacket over a white tank top paired with black jeans and black motorcycle boots with metal studs. She wore heavy makeup, with purple lipstick that was almost as dark as her thick black lashes and eyebrows.

Rancora scowled right back at the girl and was about to use a bit of negative energy manipulation to knock her down when the pendant instead crackled, indicating that this was her Wisher. "I—I'm so sorry," Rancora backtracked with a tight smile. "I didn't mean to get in your way."

The girl's purple lips curled into an angry snarl as she examined Rancora. "It's okay," she finally decided, tossing her head in the direction of the crowd. "It's *their* fault anyway."

Although most of the Wishlings pushed their way into the clothing store, several of them were loitering outside, jumping up and down, screaming and squealing. As Rancora looked from one to the next, she realized that they were almost all girls.

"Juan!" one of them suddenly called out, trying to push through the wall of bodies that blocked the store's entrance. "Please! I need to talk to you!"

"*What* are they trying to do?" Rancora asked her Wisher when she saw her rolling her eyes and shaking her head.

"Seriously? You don't know?" the Wisher replied.

"Not really," countered Rancora as she squared her shoulders and stood tall, easily matching the girl's haughty attitude. "Should I?"

"My brother Juan is in there somewhere, and those are all his wannabe—or, you know, *Juannabe*—girlfriends . . . and boyfriends," she explained.

"Oh." Rancora nodded as her pendant silently channeled a few important details to her about Juan. "You're talking about Juan Vasquez? The Internet star?"

"See?" The Wisher scowled. "You *do* know. Everyone does."

"And you're his sister?"

"Yeah—but you better not tell me how lucky I am to be related to him," the girl fumed, waving an angry finger in the air. "And do *not* tell me that you're a Juannabe Internet star just like him. I *don't* want to hear your demo. I'm *not* gonna give it to him. I *can't* help you!"

Rancora smiled to herself as she listened to the girl's tirade and thought about the amount of negative energy she might be able to gather from this mission. She had met a lot of Wishers with attitude through the years, but this one was incredibly angry—in a truly awesome way.

"Oh, I would never say any of that," Rancora replied as her pendant channeled some advice to help her craft the most effective Wishworld identity for the task at hand. "I'm actually a music producer, so I get the same annoying requests all the time. Everybody wants to be an Internet star these days, you know?"

When the girl heard that, everything about her softened—her shoulders relaxed, she stopped scowling, and her dark eyes brightened beneath her thick purple-streaked bangs. "You're a *producer*?"

"Uh-huh." Rancora nodded.

"Me too!" the girl said—and then, with eyes darting from side to side, she stepped closer and whispered, "*I'm* the one who does the production work on all Juan's music and videos. That's why this drives me *especially* crazy."

Rancora felt her pendant beginning to tremble beneath her black T-shirt and knew she was getting close to discovering the girl's wish. But before she could, a couple of Juannabes raced over and interrupted their conversation.

"*Ohmygod!* Are you Mallory?" one of the girls, who had a headful of long braids, asked.

"Yeah, why?" Rancora's Wisher replied impatiently.

"I knew it!" the other girl with the frizzy blond hair chimed in. "You're his sister! You get to live with him!"

"I *know*," an exasperated Mallory answered while sucking in her breath and rolling her eyes as she looked over at Rancora.

Finally, after drilling Mallory with endless questions, including "What does Juan wear to bed?" "What kind of toothpaste does he use?" and "What does he eat for breakfast?" the girls disappeared back into the crowd waiting to push into the store.

"See what I mean?" Mallory bristled, walking over to Rancora. "He gets all the credit for everything and I'm sitting here answering questions about the color of his stupid underwear. It's ridiculous!"

"Yeah, that would drive me crazy," Rancora replied with a sympathetic smile. "And you don't even get any of the credit?"

"No!" said Mallory, whose face was now flushed pink with anger. "I wish people could hear what he really sounds like. I wish they could see that he's not as great as they think he is—or as *he* thinks he is! I wish, for once, he would get hundreds of negative comments instead of millions of likes!"

Rancora felt her pendant pulsating forcefully beneath her shirt and a surge of power coursed through her body so intensely that it made her fingers curl into eager fists at her sides. This was her first triple wish— three times as evil as the previous ones! It was almost too bad to be true!

"I might be able to help you with that," Rancora said, her lips stretching into a confident, knowing smile.

"Really?" Mallory's eyes widened in excitement, though there was still some skepticism.

"Absolutely." Rancora nodded. "We producers need to stick together, right?"

When Mallory smiled gratefully and waited for Rancora to elaborate, the wheels in Rancora's head began to spin at an accelerated pace as she realized the significance of this mission. At last she would have an opportunity to harness the advances in technology that had come about in recent Wishworld years. With the help of the Internet and social media, the hurt and humiliation she would be able to cause wouldn't be limited to the victim's immediate circle—it could be executed on a much larger scale, potentially three times as big! And with all of Wishworld watching!

21

After discussing the finer points of music and video production for at least the next twenty minutes—all while Juan continued to chat with his fans—Rancora had successfully positioned herself as a music industry authority. She could see that Mallory already considered her to be a trusted new mentor, which was further confirmed when Mallory asked if Rancora would like to check out her home studio.

"Sure," Rancora agreed.

"Great—let's go!"

"You don't need to wait for Juan?" Rancora asked.

"No." Mallory shook her head and shot a final look of contempt at the crowd, which had thinned only slightly for a time, but again grew as more teenaged Wishlings entered the mall and learned that Juan was there. "We have an understanding that whenever the Juannabes show up, he takes the bus home."

"Cool." Rancora nodded, impressed.

Once they were inside her black sedan, Mallory cranked up the stereo and played some of her favorite bands for Rancora as she drove through one busy city street after another. Meanwhile, Rancora continued to receive useful information from her pendant about everything from the hottest and most reputable Wishworld music video producers to the latest production equipment.

"Wait—what?" Mallory gasped, nearly swerving off the road as Rancora began to name-drop. "You've worked with Ross Vegas *and* SpikeTool?"

"Yeah," Rancora replied. "But MonkeyGermz was the one who taught me everything I needed to know."

"No way!" Mallory slammed on the brakes, the tires screeching as she made a turn. "MonkeyGermz? He's the bomb!"

"Right?" Rancora agreed, clutching the edge of the dark red leather seat as Mallory sped up again. "And you know what he told me?"

Mallory shook her head and Rancora took a deep breath, not only because Mallory's driving was somewhat terrifying but also because she was about to share some information that, if all went well, would allow her to help Mallory with her triple wish. "Producers have the power to make or break their artists—and most of us are killing the industry," Rancora revealed.

"Seriously?" Mallory focused her wide eyes on Rancora as she pulled the car to a sudden stop on the side of the road. "How so?"

"We're covering everything up too much—making artists sound too perfect, not enough like themselves," Rancora explained.

Mallory slammed her hands against the red leather steering wheel and nodded. "Yes! Yes! I've been saying that for years! And I hate to say it, but that's *exactly* what I've been doing with Juan."

Rancora acted as if she understood but then, somewhat confused, tilted her head. "Why did you stop the car?"

"Oh—we're here!" Mallory pointed out the car window at a small white house with a red door.

After they both got out, Mallory led Rancora up a brick path, which divided the front yard in two and then wound around to the back of the house, where there was a smaller white building. It appeared to be what Wishlings called a garage, but when Mallory clicked on a small black device and the large, heavy door slowly opened, Rancora saw that it was filled with all sorts of musical instruments and electronic equipment.

"Come on in," Mallory said as she sat down on a rolling metal stool and positioned herself in front of one of several computer monitors sitting on a massive black desk.

Rancora took the other rolling stool and sat next to Mallory, who began clicking on various images on the monitor until a series of videos came up.

"I'm sure you've already seen all these," Mallory said as she scrolled through the images, which each had Juan's name and a song title next to them.

"Of course." Rancora narrowed her eyes as she examined the screen. "Do you have anything new—stuff you haven't finished producing yet?"

"Oh, yeah—*tons.*" Mallory clicked over to an image of a folder titled JUAN-ROUGH CUTS, which contained a list of at least fifty files. "But he would kill me if I ever played these for anyone without mixing them first."

That was it—Rancora's chance to help Mallory make her wish, or possibly *all three* wishes, come true.

"I bet they're not that bad," Rancora said. "Remember what I was saying earlier about what MonkeyGermz told me?"

"Yeah, but—"

"Well, it's true," Rancora interjected. "You have to give the public a chance to hear the *real* Juan. Weren't you telling me earlier how much you wished his fans could hear what he really sounds like?"

"I didn't mean it *that* way," said Mallory as she again scowled at Rancora like she'd just morphed into a Juannabe. "I mean, if you heard this stuff—"

Rancora smiled and tightened her fists, ready to go in for the kill. "But I haven't," she insisted. "Nobody has but you. So pick a track and put it up online. It's the honest thing to do."

"I don't know." Mallory mashed her dark purple lips together and took a deep breath.

"Don't you see?" Rancora demanded, desperate to get the mission moving. "This isn't just a chance to show people the real Juan—it's a chance to show them the real *you*, the producer who works the magic that makes him sound so amazing. Finally, you'll get the credit you deserve!"

Rancora looked from Mallory to the screen, where she could see the tiny arrow hovering over one of the unmixed videos. She looked down at Mallory's hand, positioned over the computer mouse, trembling but so close to clicking it. Rancora centered her eyes upon Mallory's fingers, mustering every bit of negative energy manipulation she could until—at last!—Mallory clicked down and dragged the file over to the LinkTube window.

As the video began to upload, Rancora braced herself for the first wave of negative energy she would collect. As soon as that video went live, Mallory's first wish—for people to hear what Juan really sounded like—would come true. But would they see that he wasn't as great as they thought? Would he get hundreds of negative comments? That would take time.

However, the moment Juan's video went live, a fantastic cloud of negative energy flowed like a black fog from Mallory and went swirling into the crystal teardrop hanging around Rancora's neck.

But that's not what thrilled Rancora the most—it was the sound of Juan's voice and the rough mix of the video that sent a surge of power coursing through her once again. He sounded *awful*—and over the course of the next several minutes, the views began to add up. Mallory's other two wishes would come true in no time. Rancora was certain of it!

Sure enough, the backlash from Juan's fans was almost immediate and the comments became more and more brutal as the minutes ticked by.

Is this a joke? asked one.

My ears are bleeding! said another.

I want those three minutes and nine seconds of my life back, a former fan lamented.

Is there any way to un-watch that? begged yet another.

I Juannabe as far away from that video as possible, someone else declared.

As she read one comment after another, Mallory shot a panicked look at Rancora—but it was too late for her to turn back. Another huge dark cloud of negative energy was already swirling around her and winding its way over to Rancora's pendant.

"I didn't mean for this to happen!" Mallory cringed, slapping a hand over her eyes in an apparent attempt to shield them from all the hateful comments Juan's video had already received. "I have to take it down—don't I?"

Rancora shook her head. "Absolutely not," she insisted. "Give it some time. His true fans will probably see the raw talent that's still there and come to his defense—plus, we need to wait until people start commenting on the production of all the earlier videos when they realize how different this one looks and sounds. You'll finally get the credit and stardom you deserve!"

Of course Rancora didn't really care if any of that happened. She simply needed to ensure that the video stayed up long enough for bad wish number three—the gathering of hundreds of negative comments—to come true. So she sat there with Mallory, waiting as patiently as she possibly could, drawing strength from all the negative energy she had collected. Ultimately, within less than an hour, it had happened. The third wish had been fulfilled and the most enormous cloud of negative energy that Rancora had ever seen began to swirl around Mallory, practically filling up the entire studio before winding into a thick tornado and diving into the crystal pendant with a final, satisfying swoosh.

Back in the Negative Energy Facility at last, Rancora shed her glimmermoth form and struggled to walk as she made her way through the fine gray mist and past the rows of moaning and wailing orbs. When she finally reached her lair in the back of the NEF, Rancora would greet all the little images of the Wishlings she'd assisted on her bad Wish Missions, which were now joined by Mallory's sad face.

But instead, she doubled over in agony. That was the one unfortunate side effect of helping to grant bad wishes: each mission depleted her—and left her feeling physically ill. Of course she should have known that granting three bad wishes in such close succession would exhaust her more than any single mission had.

Once she could walk again, Rancora marched over to a large black box sitting on her dark glass bench and carefully raised the lid. Inside, resting on a bed of velvety gray fabric, was a giant version of the crystal teardrop hanging around her neck. She removed her pendant and transferred the negative energy from the smaller teardrop to the larger one, just as she always did when she returned from a bad Wish Mission. But this time, the giant crystal began to shake with an intensity Rancora had never seen before, and that was when she knew that it had finally been filled to capacity.

"At last! At last!" she screamed with victorious delight, raising the enormous teardrop over her head. "At last I have enough!"

She had been waiting for that day—the day she would have enough negative energy to take over Starland—for so long. And now, finally, it was time for her to move on to the next phase of her plan.

22

Rancora had made the long and perilous journey to the Isle of Misera many times, but the boat ride seemed swift and almost effortless now that she knew it was only a short time before she began to destroy Starland. Under the dark shroud of night, she felt a chilling satisfaction as she approached the shore, where black water lapped at the glowing gray sand. Clutching her precious box with the large crystal teardrop inside, along with the negatite rock that had come from Mallory's Bad Wish Orb, she trained her fiery eyes at the prow of the boat to slowly guide it onto the rocky beach. Then she made her way toward the familiar path that cut through a forest of thorny, knotted trees.

When she reached the end of the path, Rancora headed straight for the Negatite Garden—an enormous glass house where she had been cultivating the plants that would be crucial in her plan to infiltrate Starling Academy. Her old friend Stella had been headmistress of their alma mater for far too long, and it had taken almost as many decades of bad Wish Missions for Rancora to gather enough negative energy to take over Starland. It was now time to perform her most challenging transformation spell yet.

As she slid open the transparent door to the garden, the entire house began to hiss and gasp, and Rancora could hear the gnarled shrubs and tattered blossoms crying out, each one begging for her to tend to it first.

"Don't worry, my darlings," she cooed after quickly grinding Mallory's negatite rock into powder and placing it in a long glass test tube. Then, making her way along the rows, she sprinkled the dark dust into the soil below. "There's more than enough for everyone."

The plants heaved and sighed, twisting and bending toward Rancora as she continued to feed them the sinister sustenance they craved.

"I know, my darlings, I know," she told them as she made her way to the back corner in search of one plant in particular. "You're ready to go on a mission of your own and *I'm* ready, too!"

Rancora walked over to the very first twinklefoil shrub she had ever planted, and bent down to check the negatite level in the pot. Her purple eyes glowed with delight on discovering how far it had come. As she plucked one of its enormous gray blossoms, it let out a twisted scream and instantly sprouted long, sharp thorns from its thick wood-like stem.

"Silence!" Rancora snapped at the plant, and the thorns immediately retracted. "This is why I've been feeding you so well, and at last you've delivered!"

As the plant curled and wheezed apologetically, Rancora gave it a gentle pat and stormed back through the garden and out the glass door. Certain that she now had everything she needed, she raced across the dusty landscape toward the cottage where she had stored the rest of the ingredients.

On arriving at the sagging wooden structure, Rancora flung open the door and ignited several candles with a silent, negative energy–fueled command. She marched across the cold black floor to a jagged tree stump that functioned as a table, and set down the gray flower next to a holo-book entitled *Negatite Magic*. Next she lifted the lid off a large container and began to examine each of the ingredients gathered over the course of her many bad Wish Missions. But it wasn't until she came to a pair of old but still sparkling friendship charms—hers in pale blue and Stella's in golden pink—that a solitary, shimmering tear began to make its way down Rancora's sunken gray cheek. She scowled as she wondered if Stella had even noticed she'd taken both halves of the charm they shared on the day she was expelled from Starling Academy.

"Enough!" Rancora roared at herself, brushing away the lone tear and dropping the charms back into the container.

She quickly grabbed the *Negatite Magic* holo-book and scrolled through until she found the recipe she had been studying for several long decades. It was finally time to get to work, and she didn't want to waste another moment. So she gathered up the container full of ingredients and the flower she had just plucked from the Negatite Garden and carefully followed the recipe, step by step, muttering the directions to herself as she did so:

1. In a simmering pot of Misera's black waters, place the hairs of at least ten distressed Wishling daughters.
2. Crumble in petals from one twinklefoil that's dried up after growing in negatite soil.
3. Melt down two charms that still sparkle and glow for a friendship whose light went out long, long ago.
4. As all the ingredients bubble and shimmer, turn down the heat and continue to simmer.
5. When the liquid transforms to a bright purple hue, *simply drink it down and become a new you!*

It took the better part of the night, but at last the cooking and conjuring were complete. Carefully, Rancora transferred the formula to a large silver mug and gazed down at the surface as it continued to shimmer and swirl. Would it really work? There was only one way to find out—so after taking a deep breath, she brought the mug to her lips and gulped it down.

Almost instantly, Rancora's entire body grew rigid and began to convulse. With arms splayed out, she dropped the mug and it clanged and clattered on the dusty ground as a thick purple cloud began swirling around her. Breathing in the enchanted fog, she felt as if she was shrinking and expanding all at once until, finally, the lavender mist dissipated and a sense of calm washed over her.

Slowly, Rancora brought her hands to her face and discovered that her sunken cheeks had become full and plump. She continued to trace the contours up to her hair, which was now tied back into a perfectly round bun and fastened with a big soft bow. Meanwhile, her tattered gray gown had been replaced with a shiny purple blouse and skirt, and she wore a pair of sparkling purple stockings and sandals fastened with glowing silver buckles. Of course, she had gone through thousands of transformations during her journeys to Wishworld, but this was different—this was the result of everything she'd been working toward!

She walked to a dusty old mirror and studied her reflection. It was both repulsive and marvelous—the purple hair, eyes, and lips and the short, rotund physique that had entirely obliterated her long, lean frame. Rancora cringed at the way she sparkled as brightly as she had when she was a young Starling. As painful as it was to look at herself, it was also precisely what she needed to see to get into character completely. So once she'd absorbed every last detail, she clasped her hands together and took a little bow toward the mirror. Then, finally, she introduced herself as meekly as possible to an imaginary Lady Stella:

"I-I-I-I am Lady C-C-C-Cordial," she stammered. "I understand you are in n-n-n-need of a n-n-n-new director of adm-m-m-missions."

Yes. She was almost *too* good. Rancora widened her eyes and beamed at her reflection—and once she began smiling, it was impossible to stop. This was bound to be the performance of her lifetime, and she couldn't hide the delight she took in knowing that the day had finally arrived. At long last, she was going to be able to put the plans she'd been making for so long into action!

23

It had been almost a year since Rancora—disguised as Lady Cordial—successfully tricked Lady Stella into hiring her as Starling Academy's director of admissions, and although most of the faculty and staff tended to avoid her, she had used her powers of negative energy manipulation to convince them of her invaluable contributions to the school. Best of all, she knew Stella well enough to say all the right things and had become a trusted member of Lady Stella's inner circle. The headmistress regularly confided in and sought counsel from Lady Cordial—and sometimes it felt almost like old times, as though they had become best friends once again. At one point, Lady Cordial had even come dangerously close to dropping her facade—but fortunately Lady Stella had been too lost in her own thoughts to notice.

Although she was eager to unleash all the negative

energy she had collected over so many years, Lady Cordial knew that she needed to pace herself. If she gradually increased Starland's negative energy levels, nobody would suspect what was happening until it was too late—and then she would seize control. So as she wandered through the school grounds in her bright purple disguise, she took quiet satisfaction in each subtle way the release of negative energy over the past year had begun to take its toll—slightly less sparkle here, a bit of student unrest there.

One afternoon, as the academic year was coming to a close, Lady Cordial decided to discharge a carefully measured but significantly larger dose of negative energy during her lunch break on the grassy banks of Luminous Lake. On her way there, she covertly took out the dark crystal teardrop hanging beneath her blouse and allowed a small gust of negative energy to escape. Almost instantly, the trunk of a nearby ozziefruit tree lost at least half of its former shine, and many of the blue and orange leaves became parched and gray.

When she reached the water's edge, Lady Cordial spread out her fluffy purple picnic blanket and sat down. As she gazed out at the azure surface of the lake, her mind suddenly flashed back to the surprise Bright Day party she had thrown for Stella so long ago—and then, as she turned her attention to Star Prep, in the distance, she couldn't help thinking about Theodore, her long-lost love. Her purple lips curled bitterly as she contemplated all that had been so unfairly taken from her, and once again, she lifted the stopper on her crystal pendant and released a slightly larger cloud of negative energy than she had initially intended. As it traveled out onto the lake, the surface turned almost as black and marvelously vile as the waters of Misera.

Ah, yes, it was all going so well! Lady Cordial closed her eyes and inhaled deeply as she savored the sour taste of a rotten cocomoon—but her enjoyment of the moment was soon interrupted by the happy chatter of two students behind her. Still, she masked her irritation with a tight smile when she turned and saw them setting down their own picnic blanket. She knew that the two young Starlings were best friends—just as Cora and Stella had once been—so although she knew she was moving a bit ahead of schedule, she couldn't resist releasing a bit more negative energy. She promised herself that she would hold back for the remainder of the day, and softly laughed to herself as the girls' conversation deteriorated into a shouting match and the tall one with the pale pink hair finally stormed off.

It had been a most triumphant lunch indeed, but it was time to get back to work. Lady Cordial had a huge pile of new student applications to read through. So after polishing off the rest of her rancid cocomoon, she packed up her lunch sack and blanket and headed back to Halo Hall. As she made her way past Lady Stella's office—the same office where Lady Astrid had so brutally and unfairly expelled her all those years ago—she did her best to avert her eyes. But in doing so, she bumped into a student named Tessa. The emerald-haired girl was one of the more accomplished applicants Lady Cordial had admitted in the past few years, so as to balance out the underachievers she'd recruited in an attempt to slowly bring down the school's standing.

"Oh, m-m-m-my," Lady Cordial stammered—a speech impediment she consistently used, along with her clumsiness, to maintain her benign cover. "Excuse m-m-m-me."

"That's okay, Lady Cordial," Tessa replied with a courteous smile.

The head of admissions clasped her hands together and gave the girl a grateful nod before heading into her office to begin reviewing applications. But before she'd even had a chance to reach the bottom of the first holo-page, she heard a knock at her door.

"Y-y-y-yes?" she called out, using wish energy manipulation to slide the silver door open.

"Oh! I'm so glad you're here!" Lady Stella immediately charged into the office and settled down in a comfy purple chair. "I came by thirty minutes ago but you must have been at lunch."

Lady Cordial nodded as she examined her former friend's face. She hated to admit it, but Stella was lovelier than ever, with smooth, glowing skin and platinum streaks in her golden-pink hair. "I'm s-s-s-sorry—I w-w-w-was indeed."

"Well, you're here now—that's all that matters!" Lady Stella leaned across the desk, her eyes shifting around nervously before locking with Lady Cordial's. "I have something terribly important to discuss with you. But before I do, you must give me your word that this will remain between us."

An eager smile spread across Lady Cordial's face. There was nothing she liked quite so much as being privy to confidential information. It was further proof that she had completely mastered her disguise and was performing her role like the true star she had always known she was destined to be. "Of c-c-c-course," she said, reaching across the desk to give Lady Stella's hand an encouraging pat. "You know you can t-t-t-trust me."

"I most certainly do." Lady Stella sucked in her breath and shook her head, fear flashing in her sparkling eyes. "But this is quite awful."

"Oh, d-d-d-dear." Lady Cordial frowned sympathetically and widened her eyes at Lady Stella in the hopes that she would get to the point.

"Yes, well . . . there's no easy way to say it, so I'll just come right out with it," Lady Stella finally said. "There is a negative energy crisis threatening Starland!"

Drawing upon every bit of dramatic training she had received as a tiny Starling, Lady Cordial feigned complete shock. "A c-c-c-crisis? H-h-how can that be?"

"I don't know." Lady Stella pressed her lips together and sighed. "It was discovered several months ago but the authorities are still working to determine the extent of the damage and the origins of the problem."

This time, Lady Cordial didn't have to pretend to be surprised. She hadn't realized that the authorities had commenced any sort of investigation. It was slightly worrying but deeply satisfying at the same time. Her plan was working: Starland was in danger and she was 100 percent responsible for it!

"Oh, m-m-my," Lady Cordial finally replied, shuffling the applications around on her desk. "I h-h-h-hope they can stop it s-s-s-soon."

"Yes, but that's just it," Lady Stella said gravely. "I'm not sure they're going to be able to stop it—so I've taken it upon myself to come up with a solution."

Lady Cordial tightened her fists beneath her desk

and choked back a disgusted laugh. It was exactly what she had counted on: the same old Stella, always deciding it was up to her to solve the world's problems. That was what she had thought she was doing when she stole Cora's ideas for ending Starland's drought. It was what she had thought she was doing when she decided to tell Lady Astrid about their sneaking down to Wishworld and about Cora's breaking the Bad Wish Orb in the Negative Energy Facility. So of course she would think she could interfere with Lady Cordial's newest plans to take control of Starland—but as long as Lady Cordial was at Starling Academy, she'd make sure Stella couldn't get in the way. Still, it would be highly amusing to find out what she *thought* she might be able to do.

"Do t-t-t-tell," Lady Cordial stammered. "What is your s-s-s-solution?"

Lady Stella stood up and began pacing around the office, stopping every now and then to sweep a bit of nonexistent dust off a holo-book with her long, annoyingly elegant fingers or to examine one of the star-shaped sculptures on the shelves. "This is the part that you must *absolutely* swear to keep between us—at least until I decide who else can be trusted," she finally said as she returned to her chair.

"C-c-c-certainly," Lady Cordial agreed.

After sitting there for what seemed like hours, Lady

Stella divulged the information she believed to be so classified, her voice barely above a whisper. "I discovered an ancient text containing an oracle. It talked about twelve star-charmed girls who will save Starland from just such a crisis."

"What? How?" Lady Cordial blurted out, forgetting her stutter as a chill ran down her spine. "I-I-I-I mean . . . an ancient t-t-t-text? R-r-r-really?" It seemed highly unlikely that anyone—even an entire *army* of young Starlings—could do anything to hinder her plans for seizing control of Starland, especially now that she had already released most of the negative energy. Still, she was ever so slightly troubled by this unanticipated and mysterious revelation.

"Yes," Lady Stella said. "According to the prophecy, these star-charmed girls will go on Wish Missions *before* they graduate—meaning they'll be able to help grant the wishes of young Wishlings, who make some of the most powerful wishes—and, assuming we've selected the correct girls for these missions, an astronomical amount of wish energy will be gathered."

Had Lady Cordial heard that right? What on Starland would possess Lady Stella to propose such a thing? How could she possibly consider sneaking students down to Wishworld before they graduated, given all that had gone wrong when she and Cora had done the very same thing? There was no way Lady Stella would go through with it—and obviously there was no way it would work.

"But S-s-s-starlings can't go on Wish M-m-missions before they g-g-g-graduate," Lady Cordial pointed out. "C-c-c-can they?"

"According to the prophecy, yes." Lady Stella's words were firm, but there was uncertainty—even a hint of terror—in her eyes, and Lady Cordial knew why. It was because of everything Lady Stella already knew about such Wish Missions, from personal experience. "But that's why this must be kept completely confidential!"

"Ah, y-y-y-yes," Lady Cordial said with a coy smile. "It will be a s-s-s-secret!"

"Correct." Lady Stella narrowed her eyes at Lady Cordial, as if she suddenly recognized her old friend— the one who had proposed the same sort of secret mission years ago. "In fact . . . this is the first time I've ever felt comfortable enough to share this with anyone else, but, well, when I was a student here, many years ago, my own headmistress told me about the first part of this oracle and swore me to secrecy, just as I'm now doing with you."

"*What?*" Lady Cordial instinctively shouted, completely caught off guard, but quickly realized that she needed to get back into character. "I mean, wh-wh-what did that p-p-part s-s-say?"

"It, too, foretold of a trip to Wishworld—an *unlawful* trip that would lead to the first negative energy ever to be released in Starland's history," Lady Stella revealed. "That trip was to be taken by just two Starlings. One would be responsible for the negative energy escaping, and the other would be responsible for helping to stop it . . . thus saving Starland."

Lady Cordial's pulse began to race; her face flushed as her rage reached a feverish intensity she was struggling to contain. How could Stella have kept such an important piece of information from her back then? How could she have let Lady Astrid hide the text when it affected Cora's fate as much as anyone else's? Of course she already knew that her old friend had betrayed her, but this treachery was far worse than she had realized. Lady Astrid had forced her to pay a cruel and unwarranted price, and Stella went right along with it!

"Where is the t-t-text now?" Lady Cordial asked, swallowing her fury as she quietly schemed to somehow get her hands on the oracle.

"Oh, it's hidden safely away in a secret room down in the caves beneath my office," Lady Stella foolishly told her. "The former headmistress left me a map with the details of its location, right here in my desk drawer, and I've made sure that the room is password protected. After all, we don't want anyone to see that text or to realize my role in all of this."

"Your r-r-r-role?"

"Well, yes." Lady Stella's eyes slowly filled with tears. "You see, I was the one who took that forbidden trip to Wishworld. I went with my best friend at the time. She was the one who released the negative energy, and I was the one who saved Starland!"

"Oh, m-m-my." Lady Cordial seethed at the conceited claim but kept her face blank with surprise. "Sh-sh-sh-shocking."

"Yes, I know—and my friend was expelled as a result," she added. "Oh, Lady Cordial! You have no idea how difficult things have been for me since that awful day."

Oh, really? Difficult for you? That was it. Lady Cordial hadn't realized she could hate her old friend any more than she already did—but now she was more determined than ever to seize control of Starland and especially to make Lady Stella pay. First, however, she needed to learn more about how Lady Stella *thought* she might be able to stop her.

"So h-h-h-how will you f-f-f-find these twelve g-g-g-girls?" Lady Cordial wondered.

"I have identified most of the ones who I believe are destined to fulfill the prophecy—eight of them are already students here at Starling Academy," Lady Stella noted, blinking away her tears and getting back to business. "But we're going to have to search through the applications you've received for the next academic year and decide who the other four will be."

"But h-h-how will we know?" Lady Cordial wondered, even though she had already decided that the entire plan was riddled with potential problems and destined to fail. She had no choice but to continue playing along.

"They'll be the girls with the most wish-granting potential," Lady Stella explained. "In fact, I already know of one extremely promising applicant."

"Oh?" Lady Cordial fought the urge to roll her eyes.

"She's the daughter of a woman named Indirra, a prominent wish scientist who just so happened to have been a classmate of mine when I was a student here," Lady Stella said, elaborating. "Her name is Sage."

"Hmmm." Lady Cordial tilted her head and scratched her double chin. Of course, she had already seen Sage's application and remembered what a strong student Indirra had been—which was precisely why she had been planning to reject Sage without Lady Stella's ever realizing it.

Alas, Lady Stella had already snapped up the pile of applications from the desk and, within moments, found the one she was seeking. "Here it is!" she declared as she began to read it. "Oh, yes—oh, my—oh, goodness! Yes, yes, yes! Lady Cordial, you must take a look at this! Sage appears to have everything we could possibly be looking for—and then some."

"How w-w-w-wonderful," Lady Cordial muttered, pretending to review the application after taking it from Lady Stella.

"Please, schedule an interview with her at once!"

"Of c-c-c-course," Lady Cordial replied softly, still staring down at the application.

Carefully placing the other applications back on the desk, Lady Stella added, "I need to run to another meeting now, but let's plan on looking through the rest of these before the end of the day—agreed?"

Lady Cordial nodded as the meddlesome headmistress moved toward the door. "Agreed," she said. "I shall look f-f-f-forward to it."

But the only thing Lady Cordial was really looking forward to at that moment was a quick search through Lady Stella's desk, a trip down to the secret room to examine the oracle, and then a journey back to the Isle of Misera. There was no way she was going to let Lady

Stella, nor twelve supposedly star-charmed girls, do anything to ruin all her years of plotting and scheming—and as preposterous as the prophecy sounded, Lady Cordial couldn't leave anything to chance. She had to make certain that if there was even the slightest possibility that any of it was true, she would be ready. Fortunately, she had plenty of resources, including her negatite garden, on her side.

24

As soon as Lady Cordial returned to her cottage on the Isle of Misera, she transformed back into Rancora and sighed with relief. Although she had once dreamed of becoming Starland's greatest actress—and in some ways, that was precisely what she had done—it was exhausting spending so much time at Starling Academy disguised as the weak and pathetic head of admissions. Alas, even after putting up her feet in front of a blazing fire and pouring herself a cup of hot rancid Zing, she was feeling more unsettled than she had in ages.

It was that absurd prophecy! Why did Stella insist on sticking her sparkly little nose into everything? Why couldn't she accept that it wasn't up to her to solve every problem or crisis that threatened Starland—especially this one?

The fact was Rancora knew that she had more

than enough negative energy to take Stella down—and although she hadn't managed to steer her away from granting admission to the four most promising new Starling Academy applicants, including Indirra's daughter, Sage, she *had* successfully cajoled Stella into also admitting another student by the name of Vivica. Rancora wasn't exactly sure how she might use the young Starling with the pale blue hair who quite resembled young Cora herself, but it was clear from her application that she had an impressive thirst for power. Ah, yes! Rancora got the distinct impression that this Vivica would be just the student to assist her in hindering Lady Stella's dubious dozen.

"Star-charmed girls!" Rancora sneered furiously as she narrowed her eyes at the fire, manipulating it into a more furious blaze. "Who ever *heard* of such a thing?"

Prophecy or no prophecy, she had come too far and wouldn't let anything—or *anyone*—stand in her way. But she needed an insurance plan above and beyond Vivica—something that would make it absolutely impossible for the girls to succeed. She closed her eyes and began rocking back and forth in her uncomfortable chair, reflecting on everything that had gone wrong between her and Stella years ago . . . and everything that had gone *right* during her many bad Wish Missions. It all came down to the power of negative energy, of course. So she needed to find a way to infect the star-charmed girls with the same devastating force. But how could she do that from a distance, without raising suspicion—particularly while they were on their Wish Missions?

One possibility after another crossed Rancora's mind—going down to Wishworld in disguise at the same time as each girl; finding a way to disable their Wish Pendants or Star-Zaps—but nothing seemed quite right. She wrapped her hands around the black crystal teardrop hanging from her neck and called on its powers for a sign. Inhaling and exhaling deeply, she waited for inspiration. Finally, she rose from her chair and walked to a pile of old holo-books that had been sitting, unread, in a corner of the cottage. She had found so many in the silver cabinet in the Negative Energy Facility, and although she had no idea where they came from or what purpose they might serve, something deep inside told her to grab these in particular and bring them with her. Still clutching the pendant, she stared down until one of them, and then another, began to glow. She picked them up and read the titles.

"What?" Rancora scoffed. "*Negatite Arts and Crafts? The Negatite Florist? Negatite Nail Care?* Preposterous!"

She was about to cast the holo-books aside, but her pendant's negative energy continued to pull at her, coaxing her to dig deeper. So Rancora reluctantly began scrolling through the pages of *Negatite Arts and Crafts* until a specific entry caught her attention.

"Ha!" she cackled to herself as she read through the instructions for fashioning Wishling key chains and purse charms filled with negatite. It sounded absurd, but the more she studied the directions, the more promising the idea became. Could such a thing really work? Encouraged, though still not entirely convinced, she turned her attention to *The Negatite Florist*.

"Hmmm," she mused, nodding as she read a point-by-point tutorial on cultivating bickering flowers— bouquets that would cause tension between any Starlings who happened to be in their presence.

She then glanced quickly at *Negatite Nail Care*, which had some interesting suggestions for mixing negatite into nail polish to give its wearer a false sense of self-confidence.

It all seemed a bit far-fetched, but something continued to pull at her, insisting the putrid projects held more promise than she realized. So she decided to give the key chains a try—which, unfortunately, required her to first rummage through a trunk at the foot of her creaky old bed. She scowled as she picked at its contents, which included an endless array of sparkly clothes, accessories, cosmetics, fuzzy toys, and other playthings from her youth. When she'd first left her family under the guise of getting help at a brighting facility, she didn't think she'd need to pack up such relics to take with her—but when she was about to toss them away, they kept floating back into her trunk. Now, at last, she understood why.

Once she'd selected the fluffiest, most sparkling materials from the lot, she sat down at her worktable and reviewed the instructions. Then, using her powers of negative energy manipulation, she began snipping and sewing together an offensively adorable star-shaped key chain.

"How sweet," she jeered at the thing as she finished assembling it.

Then, ever so carefully, she took out one of her many test tubes full of negatite powder and poured a steady stream of it inside. Almost immediately, the glittery pink ornament began to tremble and twitch—and within seconds it was glowing twice as brightly as before. It was quite captivating indeed!

So Rancora began work on another one. After she had completed all twelve, she stared down at them and clasped her hands together, eyes blazing with self-satisfied anticipation. Yes—she could see it more clearly now: the toxic trinkets would be the perfect little stowaways! She could practically picture the dastardly scene playing out in her head: The key chains would look unassuming when she, as Lady Cordial, gifted them to each girl under the guise of helping them blend in on Wishworld. Those naive little Starlings would have no clue that such tiny talismans could contain enough negative energy to completely ruin their Wish Missions.

"Perfect!" Rancora crowed. "Marred charms for the star-charmed!"

Although she had been working for several long hours and it was getting quite late, the success of her first craft project had given her far too much of a negative energy boost to sleep. So Rancora decided to take a quick peek at *Negatite Nail Care*, and mere moments later, she had gathered up a dozen old nail polish bottles from her trunk. She wasn't sure that the crusty old lacquers would be of any use now—but as soon as she began pouring a bit of negatite into the first bottle, it started to bubble and glow. Almost instantly, the lavender varnish had become better-than-new nail polish. After she'd transformed all twelve bottles, Rancora laughed happily to herself. She was already imagining how she, as Lady Cordial, would organize a mani-pedi party for Lady Stella's star-charmed students. Little would they know that their nails would make their personalities so strange that they would completely botch their Wish Missions!

Now Rancora was feeling even more energized—and it *had* been quite some time since she'd visited her pets in the Negatite Garden. So off she went to get started on the bickering flowers. As she opened the glass door and made her way inside the hothouse, her beloved plants began to rustle and hiss, eager for her attention.

"Yes, yes, yes," she cooed as she strutted between the rows, giving each plant a pat as she headed for the spot where the ones with the biggest blossoms were housed. "I've missed you as well."

Although it would be many months before she would need to enlist the services of the bickering flowers, Rancora knew it would take almost that long to ensure that they were infused with a sufficient level of negatite—enough to create tension among Lady Stella's star-*doomed* girls as they began forming friendships.

"Ah, there you are," she clucked when she surveyed the pots full of gray flowers.

Referring to the *Negatite Florist* holo-book, Rancora scrolled to the page that was still glowing, and followed its instructions, carefully fertilizing the soil around the base of each stem. As she did so, she muttered for the first time the words she would need to repeat during each visit, ultimately resulting in the flowers' toxic trans-formation: "*Bicker, squabble in your rooms, as you look upon these blooms! Smell their fragrance, oh so sweet, till it's time for your defeat!*"

As she repeated the spell and fertilized each pot with

negatite, the parched petals initially curled and cried out in pain but then began to perk up with a bright and dazzling coral hue while emitting an intensely floral perfume. It was as if they had never been infected with negatite at all—and yet they were entirely steeped in the stuff! By the time she sent them to Starling Academy at the beginning of the next academic year, the blighted bouquets would be ready to wreak all sorts of havoc, like flowery little versions of Lady Cordial herself!

Indeed, there was no way her plans to destroy Starland could possibly be diverted. Lady Stella and her pathetic prophecy were no match for the evil Rancora! She was far too powerful now.

"Good luck with your Wish Missions, star-charmed girls," Rancora cackled as she finished her work in the garden and made her way out of the hothouse. "You're certainly going to need it!"

299

PRESENT-DAY
STARLAND

Adora crossed her arms, hugging them against her trembling body as she sat on the tear-shaped bench in Rancora's negative energy alcove with Sage and Scarlet.

"Those flowers . . ." Adora stared wide-eyed at the lingering holo-image of Rancora walking out of the Negatite Garden and thought back to how bitterly she'd argued with Tessa—and how much all the other Star Darlings had argued with each other—until the bouquets had finally been removed. "We knew they were full of negative energy, but wow . . ."

"Yeah, and those key chains—and the nail polish!" Sage shook her head, remembering how she had almost run out of time on her Wish Mission and how Tessa had to come down and help her. Cassie had had similar issues, and that was after the mani-pedi party that only the Star Darlings had attended. "So that's how she made them!"

Scarlet scowled, her mind still spinning over everything they had just discovered. "Rancora is seriously twisted—and seriously scary."

Sage closed down the holo-journal and leapt to her feet. "We need to get out of here," she insisted. "We need to show this to Lady Stella—especially the part about where Rancora's been storing all her negative energy and growing those plants."

"Hmmm, I don't know," Adora said, standing up and grabbing the holo-journal from Sage. "I think we're going to have to go to the Isle of Misera."

Scarlet got up as well and nodded. "Yeah—we need to destroy that hothouse of horrors and her giant urn of negative energy!"

"Not without Lady Stella, though," Sage interjected, looking from Adora to Scarlet. "Right?"

But Adora shook her head. "Wrong. We've come this far—and these jumpsuits will keep us safe!"

Sage sucked in her breath. The Negative Energy Facility was already bad enough; there was no way she was going to set foot on the Isle of Misera, and she couldn't possibly let Adora or Scarlet go, either. "What if Rancora's still there?" she pointed out. "I mean, that must be where she's hiding."

Adora nodded as she considered that possibility. "You may be right."

"These jumpsuits may be powerful, but I'm not sure that the three of us can take on Rancora—with or without them," Sage added.

"I have to agree," Scarlet said, frowning apologetically at Adora. "We probably should go find Lady Stella and show her the evidence. Maybe she'll have already figured out a plan—but she's going to want to see this holo-journal before she does anything."

"Exactly!" Sage agreed.

Adora finally relented. "Okay, I guess that's true." With the holo-journal tucked safely under her arm, she was about to lead the way toward the front of the Negative Energy Facility. But just then, a shadowy figure appeared before them, sending a paralyzing chill down their spines.

"Hello, *Star Darlings*."

It was Rancora! She was surrounded by a dark cloud of negative energy, and the tendrils at the bottom of her tattered gray gown slithered and swirled like serpents while the high purple collar rose behind her head in a fiery blaze. When she came into full view, the girls recoiled in horror.

"I think it's time that you join forces with me, don't you . . . ?" Rancora flashed a vicious smile as she yanked the black chain from around her neck and waved the crystal teardrop in the thick and treacherous air, ready to lift the stopper and infect them all.

The girls gasped and huddled together, shrinking inside the jumpsuits Adora had made. There was no way the yellow garments could possibly shield them from the massive amounts of bad wish energy Rancora was about to unleash. Could they? She was blocking their way, keeping them trapped inside the small lair within the NEF that she had created and they had snuck into.

"What should we do?" Sage whispered under her breath. Surely one of them could come up with something—but they'd have to think fast, and her question was met with nothing but Adora's and Scarlet's blank, terrified stares.

"The rock!" Scarlet suddenly said under her breath, grabbing Adora's arm when she remembered the negatite Adora had put in her pocket earlier.

Adora reached into her pocket and was searching around on the ground for something to crush the rock with when Sage stopped her.

"No!" Sage screamed, the danger and urgency of the situation making it impossible for her to keep her voice down. "Don't mess with the negatite. It's toxic!"

"I meant she should *throw the rock at her*," Scarlet hissed.

Adora stood frozen as Rancora moved closer to her.

"Yes, yes, Adora—crush up the negatite!" Rancora said, nodding, her purple eyes bulging with fevered determination as she continued to wave her pendant overhead. "It will go perfectly with the negative energy you've been absorbing!"

"She's lying," Sage announced. Her mind-reading skills were always sharper in dangerous situations. "She's just saying that to scare us."

"You should be scared of me!" Rancora shouted, and lifted her teardrop pendant.

"All you have left in your pendant is barely enough negatite to turn yourself into a glimmermoth," Sage said, trying to call Rancora's bluff. But Rancora was in her element, surrounded by all the Bad Wish Orbs, and she used her finely tuned wish energy manipulation skills to fling Sage against the back wall of the NEF, where she landed with a loud *oomph*. It was clear that they were on Rancora's turf, that she could harness the negativity in the air and use it to her advantage.

"You have no idea what I have or what I'm capable of," Rancora roared.

Adora swallowed hard and wrapped her fingers around the rough surface of the rock, willing it to turn into a weapon. If she could turn cocomoon husks into soft stockings, surely she could turn a rock into something that could hurt Rancora, or at least distract her enough that they could run past her and out of the Negative Energy Facility. As Adora made a move, Rancora used her energy manipulation to fling Adora into the bookcase. Several holo-books fell out, nearly hitting Adora on the head.

Rancora glided closer to them, lifting the top off her pendant. Adora scrambled to get up, still holding on to the holo-journal.

"That's quite enough, *Cora!*"

There, standing behind Rancora like a Starling in shining armor, was Lady Stella, looking more magnificent than ever in her shimmering platinum gown. Then, one by one, all nine of the remaining Star Darlings stepped out from behind her like a dazzling rainbow after a storm.

"Stella?" Rancora growled as she spun around, her amethyst eyes blazing furiously and her ashen face growing even paler. "What are *you* doing here?"

Lady Stella sighed with a look of calm pity. "I didn't exactly have a choice," she replied, echoing the exact words she had said to her old friend outside the Negative Energy Facility long ago.

"But you were always too terrified to come inside," Rancora mocked. "Remember, you just hid outside, scared of these little old bad wishes."

"Not anymore," Lady Stella replied, shaking her head as she extended her arms and opened her hands to reveal the twelve crystals—each one the powerful product of a successful Star Darling mission. As she did so, a giant ring of positive energy swept around the girls—lassoing Adora, Sage, and Scarlet to the rest of the group and finally, as they all joined hands, lifting the twelve of them off the ground, along with Lady Stella.

But this time, when faced with the Star Darlings' glowing Power Crystals, Rancora didn't scream, nor did she disappear.

"Well, your star-charmed girls may have succeeded on their Wish Missions, but it appears that your Power Crystals aren't strong enough to hurt me—not inside the Negative Energy Facility!" she sneered at Lady Stella. "And mark my words: this is nothing compared to what I have in store for you next. You have no idea what you're up against!"

"I wouldn't count on that," Lady Stella replied with a wise, all-knowing smile.

"What's *that* supposed to mean?" Rancora demanded.

The two women stared each other down with intensity. Years of sadness and guilt and anger and hopelessness stretched between them. But they both knew there was no going back to the way things had once been; now they were on opposite sides of the energy spectrum, fighting for control.

"I said, *what's that supposed to mean!*" Rancora roared, causing the orbs inside the NEF to tremble.

But Lady Stella wasn't afraid, and she wasn't going to give Rancora the satisfaction of an explanation. Instead, she simply lifted her arms, and then, almost exactly like a journey to Wishworld on a shooting star, she and the Star Darlings flew out of the Negative Energy Facility. The last thing they saw as they made their exit was a slippery gray glimmermoth flying in the opposite direction.

Moments later, the Star Darlings were safely back in the Wish-House, seated at the same round table where they had gathered to celebrate the previous day. Even the holo-banner with the glittery gold words CONGRATULATIONS, STAR DARLINGS! still hung in the air above the table.

"How did you know to come rescue us?" Sage asked Lady Stella before anyone else had a chance to speak. She was relieved, of course, but also worried that the headmistress might punish her—along with Adora and Scarlet—for going to the Negative Energy Facility.

"We told her," Vega replied, proudly straightening the collar on her sparkly blue jacket.

"We were really worried about you!" Cassie added,

blinking nervously at Sage as she adjusted her star-shaped glasses.

"And I just knew something terrible was going to happen," Piper chimed in softly. "So Leona, Astra, and I went to find her, too—but the others were already there."

"Oh." Sage nodded gratefully at each of the girls and then at the headmistress.

Lady Stella smiled at Sage and then slowly scanned the faces of all the girls. "Don't worry," she said as she returned her focus to Sage for a moment. "*Nobody* here will be expelled."

"Thank goodness!" Sage replied with a sigh, and she sensed that everyone else was equally relieved.

"Now," Lady Stella continued, "I know that you've all made a lot of discoveries in the past few hours—but I have made a few as well."

"Did you discover the missing page from the oracle?" Vega asked.

"Not yet," Lady Stella replied, shaking her head. "But I did find something else—on the Isle of Misera."

"You *know* about that?" Adora blurted out.

"She has an entire negatite garden!" Sage quickly chimed in as Adora held up Rancora's holo-journal and sent it floating down the table to Lady Stella. "And a collection of negative energy!"

"What?" Cassie gasped.

The rest of the girls chattered nervously until Lady Stella cleared her throat and insisted that they try to remain calm.

"Yes," the headmistress said, looking down at the holo-journal. "I realized that the negative energy threatening Starland had to have been stored either in the Negative Energy Facility or on the Isle of Misera—the place where Bad Wish Orbs used to be sent, before it became clear that they were far too toxic and required a more advanced and secure containment center. That's when the Negative Energy Facility was built, but the Isle of Misera has remained a terrible and toxic place, to be avoided at all costs."

"So why would you go there?" Libby asked.

"I knew it was the only other place where Rancora could safely store enough negative energy to cause the sort of crisis that's been threatening Starland," Lady Stella explained. "The good news is that we no longer have to worry about that."

"What do you mean?" Scarlet asked. "It looked pretty awful to me."

"Yes! Look in Rancora's holo-journal!" Sage urged the headmistress. "You'll see where she's been keeping all that negative energy and even growing negatite for her evil spells!"

"Oh, I saw it—and it has all been destroyed," Lady Stella revealed.

"It *has*?" Sage asked.

"How?" Adora added.

"I enlisted the help of some of the top members of Starland's Counter-Negative Unit," Lady Stella explained. "Rancora will be in for a rude awakening when she returns to the island and discovers she has no reserves left."

"Can't we get the Bot-Bot guards to capture her?" Libby asked.

"Unfortunately, we cannot," said Lady Stella. "The fate of Starland rests in our hands alone."

A hush fell over the Wish Cavern as the girls looked around the table at each other, unable to read each other's expressions. All the terrible things that had happened were getting mixed up with all the wonderful things, and it was difficult to decide exactly *how* to feel—happy, sad, worried, relieved. In fact, each of the Star Darlings was feeling a little bit of all of that at once.

Scarlet finally broke the silence, looking at Lady Stella. "When did you know? I mean, about Rancora. When did *you* realize that she was Cora?"

At the mention of her old friend's name, Lady Stella's smile disappeared and her eyes filled with tears. "As soon as I saw Rancora for the first time—when we all discovered that Lady Cordial was not who she claimed to be, that she had fooled us all with her disguise—I knew that it had to be her," Lady Stella replied, her despondent voice barely a whisper. "That's why this has been so very difficult on so many levels—because I know how deep Rancora's anger and thirst for revenge runs, and yet I am also mourning the loss of the person I loved so dearly all over again."

As they listened to their headmistress and heard the sorrow in her words, the girls became equally tearful. Lady Stella had been through so much in the years since she was their age. It wasn't fair that someone so kind, whose only true mission was to help both Starland and Wishworld, could ever be forced to endure such pain and have to protect herself from Rancora's misguided retribution.

"This is also why I hope the lesson that has resonated with all of you is that there's nothing you can't accomplish when you work together," Lady Stella added.

Adora immediately looked across the table and frowned apologetically at Vega, who responded by folding her arms across her chest. Lady Stella shook her head sympathetically as she looked from one to the other.

"We all have disagreements—especially when we believe that our way is the best way—but the important thing is that we forgive each other," the headmistress continued. "It's that willingness to bridge the divide that will ultimately keep you safe and protected from even the most toxic negative energy. This is what the union of your twelve crystals represents—the promise that no matter what, you will always come back to each other and emerge stronger than ever."

Adora was the first to smile, blinking her pale blue eyes at Vega hopefully—and then, sure enough, Vega's deep cobalt eyes sparkled back at Adora with genuine respect and kindness. The rest of the girls looked around the table at each other as well, reflecting on the little disagreements they'd had, and within moments they were all shaking their heads and realizing how insignificant it all was.

"That's more like it," Lady Stella said, nodding approvingly at the girls. "Unfortunately, because of the depth of Rancora's anger, I feel quite certain that she will never forgive me—and because of that, this situation has become much larger than I, and much larger than any one of you. This is no longer about Rancora's getting revenge on one person, but about her taking control of Starland—using negative energy to frighten everyone into submission."

"But we have our Power Crystals," Vega pointed out, echoing the same point she'd made the previous day. "That's going to be enough to keep everyone safe, isn't it? We just saw how they protected us from her at the Negative Energy Facility."

"And if you destroyed all the negative energy Rancora collected, what more can she do?" Adora interjected.

Lady Stella shook her head and sighed. "Indeed, it would seem that our work here is done—but while the Power Crystals may be enough to protect us, in order to save Starland we're going to have to come up with something far greater than any of us may have imagined. As you saw, Rancora still has her bad Wish Pendant, and there's no telling how much negativity she has stored inside of that. It's the one thing I couldn't get to."

"So is that our next mission—to get the pendant away from her?" Vega asked.

"Perhaps." Lady Stella tilted her head as a mysterious smile spread across her face. "It is my hope that all will be revealed when we find the missing page of the oracle."

"But how are we going to find it?" Sage wondered with a frustrated frown. "How are we going to get it back from Rancora, if she's even the one who has it?"

"Yes—what can we do?" Adora asked, leaping up from her chair as if she was ready to go at that very moment. "We want to help! All of us—right, Star Darlings?"

"Right!" each girl replied as they all got to their feet and joined Adora.

"And you shall," Lady Stella acknowledged as she nodded from one Star Darling to the next. "Knowing what I know about Cora—and knowing what I know about each of you—I'm positive we'll find a way."

The girls looked at each other with eager anticipation. They might not have all the answers yet, but together they would do everything within their power to ensure that Rancora never succeeded in taking control of Starland. After all, they were the Star Darlings. They had already saved Starland once and they had every reason to believe that they would be the ones to do it again.

It was practically written in the stars.

The girls turned to one another, sharing and talking about the things they had learned. They didn't even notice when the light in the Wish Cavern dimmed, ever so slightly, just for a moment.

STAR

LET YOUR   INNER

Shin

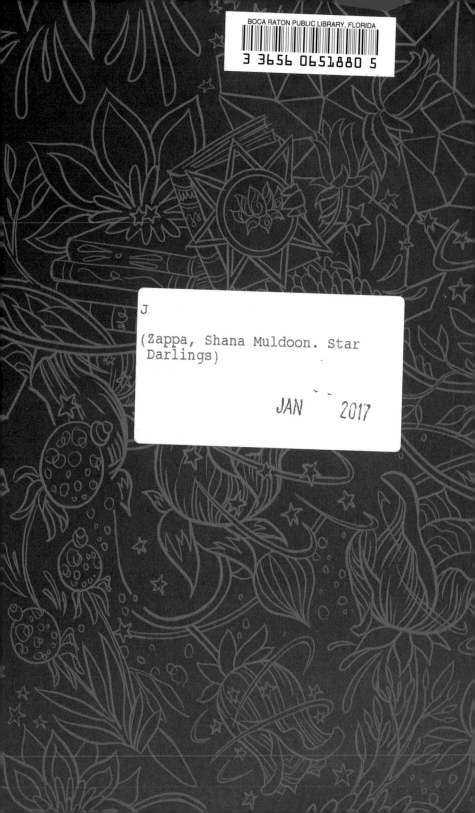